...on't remember it ...

...etails concerning the ar...

...his was a café, on the 's...

...flats, or so I imagine.

...other worked in as a teenager. It was a clo...

...my mother recalls herself working hard but be...

...and liking the place, the customers, and t...

...of garments that were sold there.

...this piece of writing was to be about the...

...my mother's stealing time & space in her...

...if it'd feel cool to be a woman I never wa...

...customer of that clothes shop, coming in...

...coat, going there, on my own, to the caf...

...street and indulge who savouring the c...

...ved there, ^pitch black, strong, far from Jamai...

...only thing I ^really remember about that café —

...ffee that was too strong for me at that...

...for as long as the coffee lasted in the pl...

...arent glass, a grown-up woman. At 16.

...place was probably connected, in some...

...s & newspapers but I can't recall in a...

...a way. It was just one large room, recta...

it smelled of wax, ?ent ????
ink and band-aids. I spent
he afternoon there 2x a month
utting together our high school
newspaper — the Lancer. Every
couple of weeks, I'd be excused
from whatever classes I had —
usually English with Laura Ker
?? our faculty advisor — ??
?? that time she was sitting at
her desk, about 7 months preg
and leaned over to get somet
out of her filing cabinet? She
reached down ?? sideways and
kept right on going till she
thwunked on the floor.
        "I'm fine! I'm fine", we
heard her say as Kathy Foats
darted to the rescue. She righted
herself in the chair and fick
her bangs back. "Center of grav
isn't where it used to be.
        At Mount Washington Press, Ma
was the "authority figure and men
he looked permanently 8 mons p?
– cigarette usually hanging off h??
owe lip as she typist for cop
wght us how to feed it thragh th

WATER

Water: A Collection of Stories

made in early 2024
as part of Sundays of Gentle Creativity

writingmaps.com

Design and layout: Shaun Levin

Cover images:
Cynthia Saunders Reed, Joanna Kania, Zurina Saban

ISBN 978-1-910289-46-4

Water

a collection of stories

London, UK

"... the writer makes books."

Ulises Carrión, "The New Art of Making Books"

"The only cure that helps everything is salt water:
sweat, tears, and the sea."

Karen Blixen, *Seven Gothic Tales*

Contents

I'll Sing You One O
PIA GODDARD

They tied her to the front end of the rope for her own safety. She knew that. They knew that too, happy now to march at her speed, the speed of I'll sing you one O, from behind her the tight response Green grow the rushes O, and so they progressed, in her time across the moor. If she stopped to look at anything at all, there was the thought uppermost in her mind that they'd arrive all at once on top of her, five big dominoes weighted down by rucksacks. Hefty rucksacks, down over her if she stopped, and the thought pushed her on. The thought of that weight on top of her, on top of her and her rucksack with its yellow leather boot hanging alone, swinging in time with their feet, I'll sing you six O, marching on. Six for the six proud walkers, coming back at her in a muffle, voices tamped into the soft mist creeping in. The boot swinging slower now, her feet in plimsoles wet and cold, hesitating, missing the other boot with its waterproof leather, its solid support. Irretrievable missing boot at the bottom

1

of the bog where she'd stopped in a previous untethered life half an hour ago, to look at the grass, the long shiny spikes of bright green marsh grass, as hard as insects, as sharp as, too, leaning in to run her hand through it, shake the voice of crickets out of it, the deception of knotted grass roots, a floating island tipping over to flip her into the bog, hearing instead of a chitin buzz the panic of the group, discordant shrieks as she'd started to sink under the weight of her kit. Then the thwack of rope on the back of her head, her hand reaching behind, grabbing the hemp and laying herself flat in the porridge of mud and weed, feeling herself move towards them, sinking as she was dragged until just her head above the surface, until she popped up by the bank, a rubber duck bobbing, draped in weeds, rust-stained, and the impatient grab of many hands reaching in to pull her out.

But that was half an hour behind her. When the sun had still been visible, as they tethered her to the front of the line, waited till she put on her spare shoes, her old plimsoles. Her yellow boot gone forever, part of the marsh now, lost in the bog. The solitary other swinging behind her, dripping behind her into the grass as they trot quickly up a slope, I'll sing you twelve O, twelve for the twelve feet marching, her leading them, up the grass onto the tor, to the post box, a metal box tucked between the rocks, to leave a card, stamp their books. I had a good job and I left, left, left, she leads with a confident stride, coming round the granite blocks to the flat top but there's neither stamp nor box up here and then they see, on the map spread on the giant slabs that they have come the wrong way, pushed their way up a different slope and now behind them, a bank of mist creeping in, marooning them at the top, catching their ankles in tendrils of mist.

To go down again is to dip into the white onto shaky ground, a rock slide down the other side where a grassy slope should have been. Shards of a ground that might slip out from under them if they are tied and tip them all to bundle down the sharp incline. One falls we all fall, I'll sing you six O, flat on their faces. They untie themselves. In zig zag steps, heels first, giant steps through the wet white, laughing at themselves and at her in plimsoles. Six of them, on they go, staggering the clitter slope together, stamping, cutting boots, ripping plimsoles and she running free down the slope, preoccupied with the lost yellow boot, saddened by it, feet skating over the rocky grey juts, bumping to a stop on the wet grass at the bottom.

Now life was all rope again. Roped. Unroped. Roped again. Back at the front. A safety thing. She understood, but wished she was at the end in her yellow boots. She was not the map reader, but at the front, following instructions, finding the line that crossed this pale soft ground rolling out around her, slowly replacing the green, the brown, the stony grey, all fading away under their feet to white, the wet white mist closing in. Soon not even their feet visible on the path, slowing down to cautious, creeping over kaolinized granite, soft under foot, up and over smooth white hillocks of clay. I had a good job, it was slow, slow, slow. White ground underfoot, white misting up all cardinal points around them, the compass needle spinning. I had a good job it was slow, slow, soft muffled footfall, but not slow enough, then solid mist, a wet wall right up against her face, full of unresolved water. Stop! Stop! her voice swallowed in the wet air. All stopped now, right in the middle of white. Waiting for the dominoes but this time just a slackening of the tether and Tight in together! and now they were a huddle, in the blinding softness of the mist pillow. Stock still. One, two, three, four, five, six, they said one after the other. All here. Again. To be sure. One, two, three, four, five, six to be certain, the feeling of breath on her cheek as they stood, waiting.

Sponges absorbing the mist, her gloved hands heavy as she poked them in and out of the white, watching them disappear, reappear, drip with water. Drip, drip, from all of them now. She bent down, felt the pull of the rope, then the bounce of her one yellow boot as they let it pay out, the weight of the group leaning back to steady her. The ground under their boots calcined white, mucky with rusty spots, dirty water dripping off them, mist water drenching them, everything sodden.

The smell of them, sharp and anxious, a brief sight of them as the mizzle shifted to let her in, all holding out their woollen hands, dipping in and out of the white, wondering at the weight of their clothes, their hats, their hair. Mist pooling under waterproofs, in the folds of jumpers, the cold creeping in as the lanolin sweat of waterproof jumpers cooled on their skin. Shivering now, cooling down, rooted to the hidden ground.

An orange light swept the mist, right through them, bleaching back to nothing, then the beam again, sweeping them, brighter and wider each time, and a distant sound through the wet, something hydraulic, closing in. Then her other boot was gone, she felt it go, cut maybe, someone behind her with a penknife, the movement was quick, weight went to no weight and the remaining yellow boot was gone and splash, there was a splash, a long way below. The boot lobbed into the white, into the water close by. Close by but a long way down. She caught the panic, a panic in all of them as they understood what it meant, where they were, the sound of that boot landing so close so far below. She took off a shoe, I'll sing me two O, two, two, my little white feet, and pushed a foot into the cloud, sliding her toes across the soft white till she felt the edge, jagged with runnels, felt the spray of the giant hose sweeping across the cliff face, the colder air funnelling up from the lake, the lake of white water. I'll sing you one foot, it's just one foot to the right, don't go right, don't go right. The rope pulling her back then loosening as her other foot bare now too makes an arc to the left, finding flat ground, I'll sing you left O, let's go left and they start their edging crab steps, an inch then another, left, left, across a space vibrating, some giant monster of a machine with orange eyes appearing out of the white, zipping past them, tugging them briefly into its slipstream, releasing them, the orange light vanishing. Right, right, right, above the grinding mechanical noise. Crabbing again a few steps. Just a few. Out of the way.

Then ice-cream, they add this to ice cream. The mist, lifting, their arms stretched out pointing at the cliffs and the lake below and the slipperiness of the spiralling quarry slopes. And paint. Stepping away from the edge. Where are those plimsoles O? There are those plimsoles O. Roped. Holding hands. Holding rope. And chalk, they make it into chalk. Following the trail of rusty drips back out. And plaster. Back over the white hummocks and onto the green. And I'll scream you one O, and they all scream together, the mist lifting over them as they creep up the slope, white peeling up the dirty grey wall of chalk, leaving them stark against it. The compass works. They lean out to look at the steep drop to the quarry floor, and the water shining.

They let it go, the long rope, watch it snake away, turn out the map to find themselves among the isobars, trace a safe path out.

Later, by the fire in the cradle of a dry valley, warm like a radiator, we're all sitting around in our knickers, clothes strewn about the heather, drying in the late afternoon sun. The sound of laughter glides on the bank of soft air sliding over grey granite boulders, catches in the bracken where six pairs of socks hang empty in the breeze. Trousers on rocks next to socks and boots by the fire drying, gloves on sticks, a bag of just add water curry, facing the flames, the food going round and round. There'll be washing later, pots and bottles and pans but now, green grow the rushes O and we sit, full and dry, wait for the nine bright shiners. Then amber light of my torch, weight of the washing up, the scour of sand on metal, cleaning and cleaning upstream in the river, alone.

Next morning there is dew on the grass, a scatter of rabbit droppings round the tents and footprints of some small animal close to the ashes. Chamomile and heath violets peep up through gaps in the heather. Dabs of pink and blue wool caught between stones. We walk upstream in the sun to fill the bottles for the day and find a dead sheep in the river, its back painted blue, hidden from the camp by a bend in the valley.

At Haytor we write postcards, squeeze them into the tiny post box, where they will wait for months, weathering in the metal, til the next group passes by and takes them one tor closer to their destination. *Looking forward to a long hot bath*.

A thick silence all the way over the last three miles. We have found a place to take off our rucksacks, spread out the map, discuss, bending our knees to sink next to a low rock, to smell a sweetness, and lurch sideways to swivel away from the swollen skin of the dead cow we were about to sit on.

"Idiot," says one of the girls, snickering. We have all given up on the map which seems to be missing a large part of the moor and straggle on to a place that should be the flat grasslands of Duck's Pool but is instead the steep side of a giant outcrop of rock. We perch on hot granite. The last of the drinking water has gone and we are arguing about the wisdom of walking barefoot. But feet swollen, rubbed raw in wet leather, soaked canvas, will never fit back into boots and we are miles and miles into the middle of a landscape of stones and long grass, endlessly repeating itself whichever way we look.

The sun has heated the air to a dry rasp and our faces are red, mouths papery. We put the rucksacks on the ground and share an orange found pressed to the bottom of a rucksack pocket. We balance a camera on a rock, set the self-timer, and line up in a row of roasted, dirty, weary walkers. The camera clicks and we walk off in silence.

Back at the house, a long time later, as I peel off a plimsole, then sock, then dead white shreds of skin, I remember the camera, left on the rocky outcrop, with its undeveloped image of us lined up against the grey granite, the blistering negative image boiling in the sun, recording the end of a summer, the end of the group. I have been dreaming of the camera for the last forty years with that image fixed in silver salts, come back again and again to that last valley, searched around every rock for it. Parting the sharp grass, poking my fingers into the soil, remembering the sheep's ropey innards, yellow, red, green, spilling out into the water and over the pans and I'll sing you one O, for her own safety. In the lay-by, posed against a backdrop of wet black granite I ask my son to take a picture. Back in the car I check the image, my face peering back framed in hair going white with the mist.

as far as I can recall it was always
When us kids   escaping the school day
When ~~we~~ visited the quarry but I know
                                       went there
can't be right because we ~~visited~~ your round
so on some days it must have been. w
                    freckled
Maybe even hot. As a red-head I was
especially conscious of hot back then bef
factor 50 had been invented. Is 'invented'
right for a chemical mixture of uv inhib
smelling of marzipan ~~and parma violets~~?
The quarry was cold because if I thought
when I was I would recognise I was
shirtless. Another girl, a few years back,
school rumour purported had slipped as
did the dare and never got to take her fi
exams. Which sort of seems an amazingly
fortuitous outcome but it's strange that no-one
actually say why. Broken arm? Broken l
Concussion? Dead? Surely someone's
brother or sister had a friend who's
brother or sister was around back then? Or
tis a tale the teachers whispered to the righ
the teachers' pet of the year, to dissuade us
visiting the quarry. Well done, the teacher'
~~Or intrigue so that we went at least~~
~~a week, just to see what it might be, and~~
~~try smoking, smoking until you were quite~~

The Bus Station

Joyce Hertzoff

A girl sat on one of the wooden benches in the old station, her legs dangling above the ground. She clutched the worn handle of a battered brown suitcase, her blue eyes staring straight ahead. The soft round face was as expressionless as a China doll, the only movement a quiver of her bottom lip.

An old woman approached. "Someone sitting here?" she asked the child, pointing to the bench.

The little girl looked up and shook her head.

The woman settled into the seat with a sigh, glancing at the clock, willing the time to fly by. Another half hour until her bus left.

"Are you traveling alone?" The child's laces were untied. "They probably told you not to talk to strangers. Believe you me, I don't like talking to them either." She sniggered at her own display of nerves then cleared her throat. "What are you? Seven? Eight?" That was the easiest of questions she had for the child.

Even that elicited no response beyond the girl's crossing and recrossing of her thin arms.

The woman waved her ticket. "I'm off to St. Louis. First time in thirty years. I imagine the place has changed. Don't you think?"

The girl tilted her head to look at her, the start of curiosity narrowing her eyes.

"I'm Mildred," said the woman. "Don't you dare call me Millie."

The last time she'd talked to a child was at Diane's. Her niece had three little girls and had to be reminded not to call her Millie.

"What should I call you?" She'd get the girl to talk to her before her bus came. That was her challenge. "When I was your age, my mama used to take me to St. Louis and Joplin, all over the state. We had cousins in every city, every hamlet from here to Chicago. Now all that's left is Diane, and me, and a cousin in Peoria, but him I'd avoid even if he lived next door."

The bus station buzzed with a multitude of conversations.

"I bet you're wondering why I'm going to St. Louis. There's doctors in St. Louis. Better than here, I'll tell you."

A slight nod from the girl was a sign she understood English, so that wasn't why she wasn't replying.

"You off to see your grandma? Or maybe you're on your way home." Everyone was going somewhere for some reason, including her bench mate.

The girl's gaze drifted down to study the tops of scuffed sneakers. A hole near the big toe was threatening to expand. The muttered "no" barely reached the woman's ears.

"You're not running away, are you?"

The silky, fine blond hair swung as the girl indicated she wasn't. The woman was afraid that if she was silent, the progress she'd made would fade.

"Isn't this bench hard?" she said. "Who on earth designed the first bus terminal, then convinced others to build them all the same."

There was a refreshment stand not far from their bench. A mother and young son were at the front of a short line, maybe six other people. From where they sat, Mildred couldn't read the sign but assumed there were drinks and snacks for sale.

"Are you hungry? Thirsty? Would you like a soda? Or perhaps chocolate milk? I wouldn't trust much else they sell. But I'm thirsty."

The child looked up, her focus straying to the stand. "Chocolate milk."

The woman looked at her as if waiting for something else.

"Please," the girl said.

She kept looking at the child.

"Mildred," the girl said.

"You watch my things, and I'll get us both a drink."

She left her coat on the seat and her suitcase on the floor and went to the food vendor. She told herself not to look back, to trust the girl, and she wondered what kind of home she'd been living in. She remembered Diane at that age, never as quiet as this one. She returned with two plastic cups and a muffin to share.

The child hadn't moved except to put her free hand on the woman's coat.

"Thanks," the girl said, releasing the handle of the suitcase to take the drink carefully in both hands.

"I brought us straws." Mildred opened one and inserted it in the lid of the girl's drink.

Watching the woman, the girl took a long sip of milk, then another. She'd finished it before she came up for air.

"Feel better?" Mildred asked.

She nodded.

Nothing added up about the girl. Who'd left her at the bus station? And where was she going? "I bet whoever you're going to see will give you plenty of chocolate milk."

The quiver was back and the child's eyes filled with tears as she looked towards the station entrance, then they returned to her drink cup. The sound of the straw at the bottom of the cup seemed to jolt the girl. She lifted the lid and looked inside then put the cup down next to her feet with a sigh.

Before Mildred should offer to get her another, a disembodied voice came over the loud speaker. "Now boarding, four thirty to St. Louis and points East."

"That's our bus." Mildred stood and took her coat and suitcase. "Aren't you coming?"

The girl hadn't budged. She shook her head. "I'm not going."

"Then why are you here?"

The woman looked around at the passengers moving toward the bus on the other side. None paid attention to the woman and the child. Mildred sat down again.

"The doctors will have to wait," she said.

They sat there in the now empty station in companionable silence, watching everyone else board the bus with their stories, the mother and child, the young man with his musical instrument, and the group of giggling teenagers. The girl took her hand, but Mildred still waited for answers to her questions about the little girl. Meanwhile, she'd watch over her like a bird over her hatchlings.

...the beer run factory boundary wall. At the school gate we changed our shoe... higher heels, our skirts shorter hems, ...tered, in time with each other, down the hill. Sometimes we veered off to the museum, to put a penny in the ... ...phon, or stare up at Scott's S... ...the quiet of the big hall. Mostly ...led up at the planetarium ...psychedelic swirls on the windows, a ...ce of smoke coming up from the ...low, we as through to start the patterns on ...dow extended back into the ... ...on the stairwell — a Beatlesesque ...ce of wondrous shapes, flower ...shall town colour inspired patterns ...yellow submarine, all slightly ... ...hind a creepy pall of weed ...m down in the depths. Staggering in ...on to find a table till a table ...e leather sofas, stare through the ...k boys not much more than 2 ... ...der than we were, who looked a decade ...yond us, with names like Spider, ...ack Mountain, long hair, locks ... ...eir works, so stoned they were al... ...ymobile, watching us with bar... ...inking eyes as we walked our re... ...tails down fast enough to cat... ...e late school bell ringing in the ...stance for start of afternoon school.

Red Sails, 1973

CYNTHIA SAUNDERS REED

When I wake the next morning, it's jumbled. Fuzzy. Swaying. Dark. I imagine a hum and then a judder somewhere far below. The Seiko glow says it's 05:42. *Photoluminescence: photons orbiting an atom excited, then relaxing.*

The Gladiola. Why do I remember this so clearly when it was so long ago? How long has it been since I thought of it? It must be a dream, but it feels as if it's someone else, not me. Who was I then? I want to go back to sleep but the dream and the memory continue to stir.

I'm on a ship. I know its name. I know breakfast isn't served until eight o'clock. *Eight bells.* How do I know this? I snuggle in, watch myself across the years, feel the movement and realise there is water somewhere below me. *No, her. Water below her.* Good, it's calm. Her head, not my head, hurts but there'll be time to take an aspirin and put hot rollers in her hair. Another time, much later, I remember, a tall man will call it Farrah Fawcett hair.

Panic. *Where is Leesa?* "'Boing, time for bed, Zebedee said'," someone said. *Someone someone someone* echoes in her head. Then someone else, white epaulettes, gold braid… was that when she first noticed Nigel the Navigator? *Who named these people?* Her head hurts. *And where is her little girl?*

Nigel with the epaulettes and two braids explained that the Chief Engineer, Kevin, a "bloke from Edinburgh" (with three braids and four kids back home) was taking good care of her.

The captain's dining table, the two Belgian cooks, and oh that fresh bread. Soon enough. Ah, the *saloon*. Wasn't that what they called it, that other place, the officers' lounge where they showed B-grade Westerns after dinner? Christopher Lee. A few drinks later and they all moved on to cribbage, invited her, taught her. A wooden board, lines of holes, cards. Two players, each with two pegs, king high. A race to amass cards – or was it points? Beginner's luck? Perhaps it was the racks of alcohol, bottles upside down with nozzles that quelled the pitch and roll, or hee and yaw or whatever new vocabulary she needed for this life afloat. "Draw a card, Aileen," the one called Radio Bob said, raising a beer glass. And she did. Who paid for all the drinks anyway? It keeps coming back. How many years?

"Who's Zebedee?" She hears herself giggle. Was she still

that silly at twenty-five? It must be her; she's the only female on board. That's funny, too. Were there no British Merchant Navy women back then? It's like a slow flood of memory washing over in ripples.

The one they call Jimmy, a gold bar on each shoulder, refills her glass, sets it down on the lipped table – "so it only slides and can't tumble off" it was explained – and says "Zebedee says it's time for the news, Miss, and you've had enough magic for one day." She alone doesn't know why this is funny so she smiles and asks. He tells her something about *The Magic Roundabout*, a television show for kids, and someone buys another round.

She and Leesa walk into the wind, toward the bow, the deck a bright green in the morning sun. Not so bright her tummy. The slight pitch and roll…. yes, that's green, too. What came after the Cointreau? She'd turned down a Drambuie. Had they really let her win at cribbage, or had she caught on quickly, *a clever lass* like they said?

Leesa's brown arms are flung out and she leans into the wind. White shorts, navy turtleneck, the cherished red Clarks sandals that Auntie Dang had bought her in the local Sukhumvit market. "I'm flying, I'm flying!" she shrieks, and races toward the bow.

"The anchor, the anchor, hurry, Mommy, hurry!" the daughter calls back, and so the mother does.

Three flying fish pass overhead, going in the same

direction. Mazdas, what about Mazdas? *Rotary engines go hmmmm*, that was it.

"Souvenir for you," the Mazda agent had said, grinning and proffering two shiny brass keychains as they'd stood watching the cars lowered into the hold by two huge cranes.

A keychain for her and one for Leesa. "You think 'Mazda' you need buy new car in America, okay?" the little man had said, nodding and blinking.

The American TV commercial is all she can remember at first except that there were oranges offloaded in Hong Kong. Yes, the Captain said, seeming pleased when she asked, the MV *Gladiola* – a motor vessel, she learned later, was one of the new refrigerated ships, built the year before in Glasgow. The harbour agent in Hong Kong had told her it would soon be filled with Mazdas to be on-loaded in Japan. *Onloaded?* Is that a word? Any decent writer would know, wouldn't she? She did now. How many oranges equal six hundred and seventy-five compact cars? She was never good at math.

"The fish are flying again, Mommy!" Leesa shouts over the wind, hands megaphoned at her mouth.

How they could breathe? the four-year-old had asked the captain. Everyone at their table smiled at dinner but no one corrected her. Grandfatherly-patient, the captain explained slowly, puffing in and out his cheeks, that flying fish only take breaths in the water, that they hold their breath in the air.

"I can swim," Leesa laughed, hands on her hips. "I can hold my breath underwater! Silly birds!"

The bread was baked daily, perfect after two years of rice and noodles. The tang of Scottish cheddar. Lots of milky coffee, even if it was evaporated milk back then. No eggs today, her tummy advised, remembering the night before. Perhaps a banana? *Yes, we have no bananas, we have no bananas today*, the officer chorus had serenaded with the final Amaretto toast.

Someone else's cabin. Whose? She stops, watches Leesa ahead, calls out to her. *No closer, sweetie.* Leesa stops, impatient, pointing at the flying fish.

There is a single bunk, narrow, long, a worktable. Small quarters but not cramped. Crisp uniforms, ready-pressed and waiting on a rail. "Valets," he'd said. "We all have valets."

A desk. A chair. "Just like Nelson sat in," he said. She wrinkled her nose. "You know, the Admiral, the British Naval hero Horatio Nelson? The *Victory*?" he added, and touched her nose, laughed.

She didn't know. She collapsed into the chair, arms splayed over its arms. "Call me Nelson then," she said, giddy, and threw back her head, shook her hair. God, she loved this halter dress. Her neighbour – former now, it hit her – was a Consul's wife and her entrée to the tennis courts at the American Ambassador's residence in the unrelenting (but great for a tan) Bangkok sun.

He leaned back on a chest of drawers, arms folded across his chest. She watched him watch her. Her shoulders, tanned, strong. She felt pretty here. And all these tailor-made clothes, shoes custom made for her to take home. *Home*. Was she doing the right thing?

Their eyes met. "I'm married," he said, suddenly leaning near, moving over her. "And it's a long way to San Francisco." His breath brushed her shoulders.

"So am I," she heard herself say, as he pulled her up and into him. It all went cloudy, but in a sweet and hazy way. Somehow, she'd ended up back in her own bed in the cabin she and Leesa shared. *Somehow*.

His name was Nigel Precious. She'd forgotten the name of just about every man she'd ever fallen for (except the ones she married) but not his. For obvious reasons. He lived at number 175, but what was the street? She knew she'd memorised it somewhere; had she seen a letter bound for home on his desk? The Isle of Wight. Years later, she and Leesa had travelled to England on a holiday, taken the train to Portsmouth and then the ferry to find number 175. An adventure, she said. The island wasn't a big place, after all, was it?

Leesa, a university senior then, was nosy-curious why her mother wanted to find a particular house on their trip to England. Aileen never told her. *Just someone we met on the* Gladiola. By then, she'd been re-married a long time to the man who liked her Farah Fawcett hair. They wandered, found the house Aileen imagined it might be and paused, congratulated their success and returned to the harbour, ate fish and chips, then caught the ferry back to Portsmouth.

"Mommy, I'm hungry!" Leesa runs from the bow with the wind pushing her from behind. Aileen catches up and they stand, facing the flying fish in the distance. They're on their way home. No turning back.

"We had a bet, you know," he'd said that pre-dawn Friday in Long Beach Harbour when she'd borrowed Marya's souped-up Chevy Malibu and gone to say goodbye. She'd only been back in California for a week. Leesa was happy in kindergarten. The *Gladiola* was scheduled to weigh anchor in a few hours.

What bet? Who? She'd asked, though she knew the answer: "The other blokes," he'd say. His fellow officers on the *Gladiola*. Who else did he know so far from home besides her?

Or was there one of her in every port and did it matter? They'd certainly never made a bet, not between the two of them. They'd made a lot of other things in those twenty-one days at sea, but never a bet. What odds could ever have made sense?

"What bet was this?" Does she sound petulant? What does she want to sound like? Couldn't they just stand there on the quay, the *Gladiola* moored down the way and taking on oranges again, the two of them wrapped around each other, willing each minute into something more than sixty seconds?

"Remember that first afternoon, Aileen, the day after we sailed from Hong Kong?"

What about it? They were bound for Hiroshima, then San Francisco, then here, Long Beach. It was an adventure. A British freighter out of Glasgow her aunt at American Steamship had arranged, all those Mazdas to be carefully lowered by crane into the main cargo hold – no refrigeration required – the crew she wasn't permitted to socialise with, the officers she was, the captain at whose table she dined, and one other passenger, her daughter.

"You and Leesa were standing on the fantail, looking toward Shantou, off the port side, and you were singing to her. We watched you from the bridge, could only just hear the words. But everyone knew the song."

The junk. It comes back easily. Their second day on board, the first at sea, and she'd taken Leesa to the stern to watch the churn of the propellers, probably for the fourth time that day, as they thrummed their way along the forested coastline of southern China. "Ewww, Mommy, it stinks," Leesa said the first time the diesel exhaust assailed their senses as it rose in clouds from the blue-

24

green sea. By the fourth time, neither of them noticed.

"Mommy, what's that?" Leesa had asked, stepping up on the bottom rail and grasping the top rail with one hand, pointing with the other.

She followed Leesa's brown arm – so like Daddy's – and squinted into the setting sun.

"That must be a junk," she said, "it's a kind of Chinese boat."

"But it's red!" Leesa squealed, bouncing up and down on the lower railing. "And it doesn't look like *junk*."

It dazzled in the distance, the setting sun glittering and then muting the image, bringing it into and out of focus. A three-master, it leaned as it reached into the wind, the colour of new brick from waterline to topmast, its sails like crimson bedsheets billowing dry.

"Not like *junk* junk, sweetie," she said, and they laughed together as Hong Kong, and the past, and Daddy and Grandma Nibha and Auntie Dang all slipped away behind them.

"Okay, what was the bet, *Precious* Lieutenant?" she said, retreating to safety in her favourite joke. She poked him in the ribs and looked at her watch. "It's time, isn't it?"

"Yes. It's nearly time, love," he said, transforming the endearment to something more akin to lurve. "Let's just say I won the bet, Aileen, and they all lost."

"Oh, come on," she said.

My god, those blue eyes, the epaulettes, the sideburns

they wore back then. She might not remember that street name, but she'll never forget the epaulettes and those eyes.

"I won. Fair and square, as you Yanks would say." He pulled her close and hummed into her hair, then whispered the words. "*Red sails in the sunset, way out on the sea…*"

Something stilled in her. There was nothing else to know, nowhere else to go. The *Gladiola* would weigh anchor, bound for Hong Kong, its navigator on the bridge and all those rotary engines in the hold, waiting to hum. She remembered the lyrics, too, but she'd skip the next line. There could be no "come back to me."

"*Swift wings you must borrow... make straight for shore,*" she whispered instead.

He worked at a smile. "Aileen, I only wish..."

"Shhh," she said, holding an index finger to her lip and smiling because suddenly she could. His eyes followed her hand as she reached into the pocket of her sweater, and then held her closed fist upturned between them.

"This," she said.

He opened her hand with both of his and there lay one of the shiny-new Mazda keychains.

"Take it," she said, and he did. "Now all you have to do is say *hmmmm* like the Mazda from time to time, okay?"

When he smiled, she turned away.

...st someone something they were not prepared
... Vera was frighteningly often called
... though she thought she had hidden beauties
... was difficult. She needed attention. She change
... could own truth. She could sleep sometimes.
...ished to be named to Vita. The kind of woman
...ressed in white and lace and had gloves
... But because she was so often ~~changed~~
... people thought anyone could have her —
...free. Except that Vera always cost you
...thing you least wanted to pay. It
...believed each person contained a secret
...could exhume from its dirty grave.
...had written a story of a
...net, Verushkin. which had two
...is and no moons. It was always
...ing on Verushkin. The inhabitants
... no idea what love was. Until they
...it a cave and discovered sleep. At
...it, the creatures slept ~~extra~~ for weak
...make up for their sleepless lives.
...en they stumbled out, confused with
...ams. What was this other life the
...amel leads? ~~It~~ In dreams, they
...w, they interturned limbs under
...a bearskin rug, they had children +
...t them and found them again the
...other evening. No one ~~could say~~ said.
...themselves in dreams, "this is not true."
...they understood, that ~~come~~ ~~it had~~ contradictory

riods. If they came at the end of the
any carol and I would go to mine
road and play music. When we s
... we'd go to hers, steal her m
ags and smoke in the front room.
asleep upstairs as she worked night
hospital as a ward nurse. We'd
hon she came down and ask us if
en smoking, in tandem we'd clen

My other main refuge was my dra
eachers' classes. They were held in
chool, in the hall. I'd sit against
wall and watch and enjoy the youngster
ing improv and each;

Or, I escape under the stage,
... she'd had a massive wardrobe
uilt, for costumes and props and
r productions. There was a ket
for only a drink.

Sometimes she'd drop me hom
in her car, I heard on the grape
t my class mates thought we we
... an affair. Unwarranted kind
... we weren't. She was very supp
... me, still is is.

Opposite where I lived was the fur
... and my friend lived there, I'd go
sometimes after I'd been dropped off. He
... parents by their first names. My m

Elektra Crashes, No Survivors

RACHEL WOLCOTT

Corals and barnacled whales make poor witnesses and the anemone will not clock a vanishing woman. Sea fans, spiny sea slugs and an octopus may detect a woman in a machine sinking through the waves but they wouldn't necessarily take note. She's not yet a morsel consumable or absorbable. They will feed on her once she settles and begins to dissipate.

We want her to be alive because from a human point of view dissolving is not a satisfying ending. We want rescue, perhaps by a fisherman in a dugout. He should have black tattoos and a hook carved from bone, perhaps some basket traps. The heroine needs more obstacles before she reaches her destination, triumphant. She needs to fit the stories we know already, like Robinson Crusoe, maybe the Donner Party on their way to California, if following a darker path.

In Amelia's case we suspect the Japanese captured

her (and by suspect, we mean hope). There is dim footage of a woman who could be her, but we don't know. We continue searching. The disappearance becomes an obsession. We want to know. Technology should make everything findable. We don't like messy endings.

We want to track Amelia and raise her like a shipwreck, for her bones to be forensically examined, a 100-years-late post-mortem performed. That is if there is anything left. There might be a bone or a belt buckle. Perhaps her wedding band is nearby. Creatures may have made a home in it.

(There was a man, Noonan, who in historical terms, vaporised.)

Dead whales sink. A young humpback whale was travelling 100 miles off the California coast. For a whale, that's about 200 breaths, a single sad song or two happy ones. Not far for a whale. It is 7,000 miles away from Amelia, many hundreds of breaths and songs both happy and unhappy.

Black and white missiles hone in on the giant baby, grey and awkward swimming alongside its mother. She is graceful, strong, an ecosystem clings to her. The calf rolls playfully and waves its flipper to gesture: Here I am. But within seconds the orcas divide the calf from mother. She wheels around to protect and rescue, diving and lashing. The orcas fend her off, biting her tail, her blowhole. Blood flows from her, but they cannot kill her, so they turn to the calf. Life leaks from a hole in its belly but still it scrambles to free itself from the orcas latching onto its tail, ramming its weakened body. Every movement mustered is hope, but it is near exhaustion. A breath leaves it involuntarily. The body deflates.

The mother churns the sea, anguished and plunging through the foamy swell. She turns on her side feeling the breeze with her fin and then slaps it against the surface. She smashes her tail against another wave and propels herself North. She has ploughed this water before, when she was lighter. She calls out her grief.

The carcass sinks. Blood mixes with sea water. The calf's lifeforce ebbs as the water darkens. The creatures that travel with it, adapted to it, are still alive, but will not survive the permanent habitat change. Animals take bites as it drops and drifts. Hagfish cling to the bones, wriggling and eel-like. The last of the calf sinks to the ocean floor. Hold a light up and it's dusty, but at that depth the pressure bears down compressing the bones, flattening them into the sediment. The remnants of a feast pulled down into uncharted subaquatic waters, darker and dead silent.

Amelia falls and drifts. Her broken body snags on a sea mount, an incomplete peak, an almost island, ripping her blouse, now billowing, on a coral fan. Her head clings to a dreg of life, the last puff of air. She feels nothing and her gaze trails inward, backward, not taking stock, not regretting.

The plane soars tinny and glinting. Her photograph is sepia newsprint. Ticker tape and confetti flood upon her reducing visibility. She is in Atchison beholding the prairie heat talking to her grandmother about laundry and harvesting carrots. She flips. A whirlpool rises in the wake of her sinking plane, ripping off her cap and goggles. She drives a yellow car cross country. She tries school, dabbles in nursing. A thud against the mount slows her. A brief flash of a man, boys. She stares into a giant camera. Someone dabs her cheeks and forehead with powder, helps her into new clothes. There is a typewriter and then a plane, the din of the engine, another plane, clouds, agricultural patchwork, lakes and rivers, the sea, the ocean. Nothing.

Her breath had stopped as she fell from the sky. First from fright and then, when the plane hit the water, her neck sheared by metal fragments. The windscreen exploded, gauges and instruments pummelled her face and whipped her neck. Her eyes roll and bulge. The ocean pulls her from the plane into the blue water and through a school of silver fish that scatter in panic but then regroup. A cloud of pink jellyfish sting her body. She doesn't make it to the ocean floor. A rock and coral hammock, hanging off the slope of the sea mount cradle her body, sway it to the ocean's rhythm, offering a feast to gaudy fish. An eel makes the ribs its home for two years before it disintegrates, each bone peeling from the spine and sinking. Picked clean long ago, the head vanished. The rest scattered indistinguishably atom by atom.

The wounded blowhole healed years ago. It's one scar among many nicks and gouges. A propellor slice on the dorsal another orca gash in her side. Barnacles, now enormous and crater like, ride along with the elderly humpback. She moves with kin, but alone. There are animals out there who might be her offspring, but that isn't how she relates to the ocean. Instinct and hunger move her along watery lay lines. North, south, north, south. North.

The whale feels kin breath around her even in the raging Kodiak seas. She chirps wanly, another female responds. They take shelter with others, riding along with the summer storm beneath a sea water meniscus. Above, fog and foam form a cyclone. The whales exhale and snort, their long fins reaching beneath them into the cold they do not feel.

When the winds drop, they hunt. She drives deep and circles back to the surface, bubbles trickling out of her blowhole. There is enough breath to create a bubble wall. It's a whale's fishing basket, trapping fish and driving them toward the whales lurking near the surface just outside the bubble ring. They dive to meet her as she rises and together their giant mouths gape like waterlilies unfolding in the morning sun. They push upwards, the fish filling their mouths. Sea water drains through baleen and their rubbery gullets wobble with the catch.

Shrewsbury, UK

Costa Rica

Barcelona, Spain

Casablanca, Morocco

London, UK

Gdańsk, Poland

Never Mess with a Witch
HOLLY WOODWARD

Once upon a strange time on the slithery steppes of Russia, you might have seen the Siberian witch Baba Yaga aloft on her broom. You might have spied her house as it skittered about on skinny chicken legs. Yaga called her shack Dada. The house had a mind of her own – not a bright one. Frightened of most everything, she fluttered off when the witch swooped in.

Yaga shook her knobbly fist. "I could put you into a stew."

The house shuddered and knelt for Yaga to enter. She banged pots and tickled the oviduct with a feather duster. The hut nestled in sweetgrass and cooed when she laid a great azure egg. Yaga snatched it and whipped up a soufflé with fiddlehead ferns.

Yaga lived in exile since that banquet brawl in Moscow where she had not won the Pushkin Poetry Prize. An ode to a tractor took the honors. Yaga had ripped off the judge's toupee in the scuffle, and the trophy lay dented under the toppled podium.

After the brouhaha, she flew to the woods and lived with her broom. Broomhilde didn't do housework. "Floors are beneath me."

In the long winters in the woods, Yaga sang her poems alone.

Roses smell,
Violets shrink,
Love is hell
Is what I think.

You're a fool,
I am stupid.
Long may he rule,
Our great leader Cupid.

She sent her poetry book to Moscow and received a one-word reply: Treacle.

What's so bad about candy?

She made a hive hat for the house and ran a spigot down to the kitchen window. She lacquered the parlor in gleaming taffy and fashioned a chandelier out of rock candy. Some say that Baba Yaga lived happily ever after but, kiddo, that's a myth to fool you into dozing off.

Wake up!

One day, the Katerpillariski Town Council pasted a notice to the hut's ass that forbade houses on legs.

Yaga ripped off the paper. The house squawked.

"I hate people." All the worst qualities of pigs without the tasty bacon. Bacon was her favorite sin.

The People's Commission for the Indoctrination of Witches and Seizure of Houses on Chicken Legs in the name of Vladimir Ilyich Lenin, Kumelabuga Collective, Kapustochka Oblast, SSSR, sent a posse and surrounded the hut with chicken wire. Dada's cockspurs kicked free and she flew to the mountains.

The politicians had to be smarter than the hut, which was challenging for them. The committee of ten regrouped as the Brigade for the Reclamation of Wayward Witches in the name of etc. Seven men set off. Never to return. The seven pigs who wandered into the commune were slaughtered and hung to cure.

As the three surviving members gobbled bacon, one comrade said, "Let us lay a trap to lure the witch."

"What do witches want?"

"Children?" "Give them mine," snorted a wife frying pork chops.

Men shoved their young toward the woods, then celebrated with a vat of kvass. As Dada the hut pecked her way past the bewildered children, the witch glanced up from her desk.

Although she loved children, nicely sautéed, Baba Yaga was scared of them. Terrified. She'd been a child, once. At six, she'd jumped off the roof and broken both legs, which is why she flew a broom and had a house on legs.

The kids called up to her, "Help."

She shouted down, "Run, I'm a dreadful witch."

"But maybe better than Krauts?"

She grimaced, then lowered the ladder. They climbed up and crowded her kitchen. She assessed her catch. All the scrawny children together in a cauldron would not have made a meal, even boiled overnight, with a sack of salt.

She served them snow drizzled with golden honey and they balked.

The children gasped at the palatial candy parlor, the rocking horse speckled with caramel and nougat, the curtains striped ribbon candy, and the sofa stuffed with Turkish spun sugar. One boy licked the praline lampshade, a girl nibbled the chandelier hung from the grumbling gizzard, while toddlers sucked the lollipop banisters. Her home crumbled. "Are you happy?" she called to the children.

"Yes." They hung their heads.

Happiness was not soviet. At school they studied Miserable Maths, Desperate Soviets in History, Gloomy German. They studied *Horrible Enemies Who Did Us Wrong and How We Made Them Even More Unhappy*. They took dictation in wretched Russian classics like *War and Peace and then Immediately More War*. Recreation was a battery of dismal games in which eyes got poked out. The best part of the day was glum lunch.

Koba, the town scamp, gnawed the sofa's toffee legs. He reached up to Baba. "I love you."

"Love!" Yaga bared mismatched teeth.

Love was sticky.

Meanwhile, the town formed the Committee to Combat Capitalist Harridans and Hooligan Children.

But their war on the witch was interrupted with the German invasion. Panzer tanks churned wheat fields, artillery burned silos. Screams human and inhuman. The town houses were sitting ducks, but Yaga's skittish hut fluttered helter-skelter through the woods.

Annoyed when her tea glass shattered, the witch flew by moonlight to the mountain to survey German positions. She loaded the barbed wire by her house with burning coals and dropped them on the Germans.

Panicked soldiers watched the woman on a broom nosedive their camp. Tents went up in flames and gasoline depots exploded, burning tanks. They called her the Harpy of Deaths. After a few night-witch visits, they fled.

She tried to shoo the children from her ramshackle hut, but they clung to her ankles and Broomhilde.

Stalin awarded Baba Yaga a medal for killing men. *Now* the townsmen cheered. She knew the one good thing she'd done was save children, measly as they were.

At the ceremony, she threw the medal in the dirt.

Spectators hissed, "What a witch!"

The Soviet Armed Expeditionary Force for the Capture of Rapscallions with the Further Aim of Rehabilitation in the etc., came to the decrepit house, but Dada turned her back.

This is a Russian story so the tale can only end unhappily.

It could happen that the parents fall into a trap set by the kids. As the parents starve, a child might let out a lone sob.

In the official state version, the hut is boiled into soup to feed the masses, but that is a fairy tale, my friend. No one could ever catch the chicken hut.

The witch might go to the town and say, "You can have your brats back if you leave me in peace."

After heated debate, the parents agree.

Dragged back to their hovels, the ruffians wail, scream, whimper, howl, sob, etc. They'd bite off the restraining ropes, but their teeth are rotten – that'll suit them for bureaucratic work when they grow up. Now, they're slavering sycophants, bottom feeders in the pecking order that serve the voluminous, mustachioed walrussian leader as he bellows. No one understands his slurred speech, but they clap like seals. The first to stop will be shot.

In the woods, the hut snuffles in her empty nest. Broomhilde rests her frazzled head in the corner; she hopes to sweep cobwebs for the rest of her life. Yaga stares out the window. She's even more terrified of children now. They rip your heart from your chest and leave you bereft.

She watches snow darken the sky. The white fluff turns the air black, like magic. Under cover of snowfall, a hare bounds across a field, tracing a cryptic script. The owl perched on a bare branch hears the furred feet cross the deep snow and unfurls her cold talons.

all the places that weren't
chool were som.. the places
ranted to be except. the ten...
ourts on a friday night or t...
arks where kids smoked we..
the monkey tree. & I li..
ce cream - cherry Garcia - I
liked cds. I liked a goo..
ngel, not one of the shitt..
ubber ones from the cafet...
sold for a dollar. you did..
ven get a plate. I'd go
I went to places
could get these thin..
but I wouldn't stay. —

Except for the records.
Thwap, thwap thwap, I &
filed through the registe..
ila boxes. looki..
funeral home   cakes My mom

Holly tree   snow day   we have
diy under wl   cake   people
ve stage please don't cut the...
car accident
cake.   friends'
sweet pan Range winter Mom made
cake stanley... a disaster
from J mix → cakes   names..
cake   we di..
kinds ?.   cake

Pyramid

Ann Tudor

As you lie in your bed at night, nearly settled in sleep, just your own whisper with you, you wonder when he'll visit again. Will it be tomorrow?

You lie waiting. Turned on your side, as best you can, so you can see the door. They ask why you don't want to look the other way, out of the window, and sometimes you do, when he's just been and you know he won't be back for a while. Then you can look and see whether the day is grey, whether its late in the afternoon or earlier in the day. You can't be sure of the time when he's with you but after he's gone you fall back into the lull of this place.

He'll visit soon. You know he will. He'll come to replenish the bowl of fruit on your side-table, the pyramid of pineapple, kiwi, blackberries, the figs he brings when he visits. They'll be there when you wake in the morning. Blackberries of autumn afternoons and purple lips. Figs stolen from the birds at dawn, skins dark as twilight, yellow flesh protecting pink seeds.

He'll come silently into your room, the only noise the echo of chatter from way down the corridor. He's not like those others, arriving so swiftly they barely have time to open the door. Rarely closing it once they're in the room, each with their cheery calls of instruction. Exhorting you to an action to fit the timetable of this place. But you know, they're like you, wanting to see what he brings. Last time he left a spray of redcurrants, baubles hanging, as in a spider's web. "Better for jelly with a lamb chop," one of them said. You smiled, thinking of meals eaten together, of bold red wine, rioja or tempranillo. Redcurrants more a delight to the eye than the palate. But a pleasure no less.

His visit will start with a quiet knock. His head will peep round the door to check you're there, awake, ready for him. And you will be, of course you will be, woken as you are when he opens the door by a distant laugh or the clang of a saucepan from others in the building. You'll smile, wave your right arm, the one you can still lift from your side. Its stiff and aches, but he needn't know that. You'll look at him, keeping that smile, hoping no one else will come in now he's here. They never do, although often, as soon as he's gone, one of them will barge through the door, asking if you're okay.

"I'll call if I need you," you say, remembering to add, "Thank you."

What they really want is to see what he's brought. There's no need for them to straighten the curtain or wipe the table. They go on a bit sometimes. You got a bit cross at first but now you quite like it. Them as excited as you. Like a few days back when they were making your bed. They'd got you balanced on a grey plastic chair in the corner of the room. At first you were more worried about toppling over than listening. You'd rather land on your left side if you had to fall. That was jiggered already, didn't really matter. Not that they cared. On and on they went mithering about peaches and nectarines. To be fair you could see what they meant. They're nearly the same but not. The shiny smooth skin of a nectarine, the fur cladding of a peach, often peachier in colour. Well, it would be, wouldn't it, the one said. Did they taste the same? You can't really say, the other commented, every piece of fruit you ever eat has its own taste, doesn't it? You nod in agreement even though you prefer peaches, something about their soft down, reminding you of the soft fur of your cat way back.

When he walks into the room, he'll say something like: "I've brought you more fruit. Pleasings for each day. As you deserve." You'll feel the wish of his light kiss, given in silent promise. Hope flutters, pale and downy-soft like the skin of an apricot. Today's pleasing might be white melon, flecked yellow and green, stripes of a tiger kitten, skin smooth, polished like a much-prized conker. Eating melons with him is your favourite time. He cuts it for you using the knife he always brings with him, slicing through the core, scooping out the seeds, discarding them, digging a spoon into its flesh. No knife needed now, the fruit's softness yielding to a spoon's blunt edge. Juices spilling down your chin, drops slithering further, into the napkin he holds.

Last night as the sun fell below your windowsill you thought about blood oranges. The sun could have been an orange, a perfect spherical brassy orange, the red of rose mottling its skin, giving its name. The promise of sweetness, tinged with acid sharpness catches the back of your throat as you suck on the wedge he's cut for you with that special knife. More juice to tingle down your chin, drying in your warmth.

And he's right. You do feel better when you've eaten his fruit. You seem to be able to think more easily, breathing to his rhythm beside you. You eat his fruit, cut with his mother of pearl fruit knife. You watch him as he slices through an apple or a cherry and then, using the pointed end, he takes out the stones or pips. You're sure the knife would fit perfectly into your own hand. When he's gone you close your eyes, curling your fingers towards your palms, creating a space for it. You feel its smoothness, its grain running across the top edge. He talks when he's with you, no gaps that you need to fill. His chat is about what he does each day. Morning swims at the lido, a trip to a coffee shop, lunch with a colleague, television programmes and films he's watched.

Somehow, when he's gone, you can't remember how his voice sounded. You aren't sure if this should worry you. You might sit for a while, trying to recall this sound of him. Does his voice have a depth to it? A bass sound, skimming vibrations below the surface of your consciousness. Or is it higher pitched? No, you're sure it's not but however hard you try you can't think how he sounded as he talked. Now that he's no longer with you, coaxing you to eat the green jellied kiwi with its crunchy black seeds, to savour the popping blueberries, which you squish on your tongue. Now it seems his voice barely existed.

He always makes sure, before he leaves, that he's emptied his basket, checking for smaller items, for forest purple cherries or whiskery raspberries, red in summer, gold yellow in autumn, searching for these or similar morsels that may be tucked out of sight. Turning it upside down, shaking it, smiling as he does this. Your only thought is that this is what he does before he leaves. When will you next see him? You don't ask this, as he picks up his mother of pearl knife, wrapping it in white tissue and putting it in his bag to take with him.

When he's sure that all he has brought has been delivered, he will spend some minutes arranging it, in the oval white bowl in the centre of the table. The first time he came he brought the bowl with him, a wide shallow bowl, a perfect foil for the glamour of pineapples, plums, bananas and mango. When he's gone you look at the fruit he has left. And most times the desire to eat it seems to have left with him. A tall thistle headed pineapple might sit in the dish, tempting with its sweet ripe smell of candyfloss and roller coasters. But how could you eat it without his mother of pearl knife to cut it?

This fruit he leaves has its own demands. You wonder whether he thinks about this as he drives away. You do, for almost the moment he's gone it starts to worry you. Bananas needing attention while they're still ochre yellow, before they blemish with brown spots of imminent decay. A green apple to be eaten before it lets off its faint cleggy smell, announcing yesterday's ripeness. Cherries, their skins wrinkling brown, like the liver spots on the back of your hands. They try to help, coming into your room, saying you mustn't get in a state. If they find you crying or curled up under your bed clothes, your skin damp and sticky, they wash you and brush your hair off your forehead, settling you as best they can. They know what's worrying you and they try to help, going through the fruit in the bowl, taking the pieces you've missed to eat before their best. Arranging what's left.

Throughout each day you watch the sun, then its shadow, as it passes across your window. Some days it looks like that blood orange, other times it's the reflection of the chrome yellow sphere of one of his pimpled grapefruit. Each night as it sets you wonder, in that last moment of day, where does he go when he leaves you? How long has it been since you last saw him. Twenty-four hours or twenty-four days?

When he doesn't visit you wonder how you will eat the fruit without his mother of pearl knife. If you ask, they'll help, cutting the white butter pears or Irish green apples. Like him, they cut small bite-sized portions that you lift from the plate to suck or nibble, your right arm strong enough for this. They might peel a tangerine for you, pulling off its stringy pith, separating the sections, pressing each one to make sure there are no pips. If you don't want to ask them, then there's always a strawberry to pick from the bowl, holding it by its spiked stalk, tugging at its flesh with your teeth, its light juices sticking to your lips. Or you might prefer a dark purple grape, dangling on a stem, so cleverly evolved for his purpose, holding these grapes together in his display.

Each day you eat as much as you can, knowing that in the morning, when you look from your bed to the table, you'll see the fruit is still there. Is there more or less? You're never sure. It must be as it was when finally you slept, but it doesn't always seem like it. But he wouldn't visit in the night. It must be as it was yesterday, you're sure it is. You'll start looking for something small and soft, perhaps a blueberry, refreshing after a night of dreams and slack-mouthed breathing.

They come to your room early each morning, the

helpers, two of them to turn you, wiping and rubbing you into another day, rolling you from one side to the other, always careful with your leg on the left side, the useless one, pinned at the hip, swaying as you walk, kinking away from your body, willing itself to mirror the angle it assumed when it broke your fall. The time he came because someone called him. When he brought you here.

Before that you would buy your own fruit, on your daily trips to the shops. You would talk to people on the bus and in the shops. You would walk along the beach at dawn and again at dusk, meeting fishermen at the far end of the bay while they sorted their haul, letting you have a couple of sardines for the cat. Your cat who kept you company because, after all, he was busy back then, and you needed someone to talk to late into the night or at those odd times of day when you took a break from the marking of time.

Back then he'd phone on a Sunday, late in the day, so late you didn't feel you could say: "Come over, come visit me."

Not that you would ever have said that.

At least since he brought you here, he visits, bringing you his gifts of fruit.

Sometimes you look at him in the mirror on the wall opposite your bed when he's got his back to you, when he's picking something from the bowl, a spiced brown date maybe, to be cut through with his mother of pearl knife, the stone removed before he passes it to you. They say you see things the other way round in a mirror. When you look at him you notice movements he makes that you don't notice when he's turned towards you. The long-forgotten tilt of his head, the upward flick of his jaw or the swing of his hands as he speaks to you, describing a movie he watched last night or a new car he's about to buy. When you look at him in the mirror you can ignore that he seems to avoid looking in your eyes, the way he does when he's in front of you, facing straight at you. You know you should be used to this by now. After all it's as it was back then, on the occasional Sundays when he visited, before all this, when his conscience unbalanced the neatness of his commitment.

But it's not the same now, you're sure it's not. Because these days he comes to see you often. You know because each day the fruit is there, ripe and plentiful, carefully arranged. When they come in to lift you, whoever's turn it is - there'll be two of them, working in pairs as they do - they'll comment on what is in the bowl that day. They'll smooth the sheets, as their hands might caress the skin of the melon, shaking your pillows, as if to scatter pips from the juice of an orange, stroking your hands, maybe touching your cheek too, something he misses to do. You wonder if they notice.

When they're finished and at your door they'll turn and smile at you as he would smile as he leaves you.

They'll close out their noise, the hubbub of this place and you'll lie back comforted by the cool bedclothes and the glimpse of the downy skin of the perfect ripe peach which he placed on the top of the pyramid of fruit in the bowl.

The Electrician's Wife
SJ LYON

It was on her way down that she started to doubt the wisdom of gardening at this time of day. Finding the shears had exhausted her more than she'd expected, hunting for them in the cupboard where the carers had jammed their equipment, folders of notes and boxes of disposable overshoes. She gripped the rail with her other hand, her knees thrumming angrily with every step. Other people her age talked about their joints "protesting," but the description struck her as unsatisfying. It was as if her body had moved into a menacing, uncompromising stage, refusing to concede until she was defeated.

In her pain, she wondered what the new people downstairs would do if she knocked on the door and asked for help. When the young man was living there, she wouldn't have hesitated. He had promised her when he rented the flat out, that he would find her some nice people as new neighbours. He told her it would be just like he never left, that he would be back all the time. He told her he would cut back the rose bush for her, knowing how she found it harder and harder to stand for a long time, even if she could mostly use the shears still. But here it was, late into the summer, July already, and the roses left undone.

It wasn't right, she told her husband, how the new people never said hello. They smiled, polite, tight lipped, but always as if they were desperate for her to disappear. They seemed annoyed to find themselves in the hallway at the same time as her, though she had just as much right to be there as they did. She knew there were two of them and had spent some time trying to figure them out. Were they students? It seemed likely, both dressed so similarly and strangely, bright clothes that wouldn't look out of place on a child but in adult sizes. One was a woman, but whenever she tried to remember which one, they blurred in a whirl of glasses and hair and rucksacks. There were more and more like them now. One Saturday, she'd gone into the petrol station around the corner to use the toilet, only to find someone had turned it into a bar with music. She'd stood on the cement floor for what felt like a long time as the crowd parted without a word, letting her struggle to identify the person to ask. So young and loud and self assured-she was certain she hadn't been like that when they moved into the street, their first proper home in England. They'd moved so many times in the early days. *It's not our neighbours*, her husband pleaded.

It's people who come from outside to cause trouble. From Wodehouse Avenue to Pennack Road to Lisford Street they trailed spray paint, bricks, notes. A landlord's son who, after they complained about the lightbulb in the hall being out for weeks in a winter's darkness, locked them in and taunted them for a whole terrifying day. They always smiled first, after that, careful not to betray the English to themselves. It's been years since she had made tearful threats to go back home, long enough that there's no home to go back to, but then where had these two come from if not from outside? No. She could not knock on their door.

A few steps from the bottom, her right leg stiffened and refused to yield. She dropped the shears to grab the rail with both hands but skidded those last wretched steps and fell before she could breathe. Pain bloomed everywhere, in bright hot bars on her back and head. She filled the corridor, all hips and legs and flesh – her body too dangerous to tackle alone, and for several long minutes she submitted to this fact. The shears (now hated, humiliating) were still on the step where she should have been. Shadows played across the glass of the front door from where people passed outside. The late light she was meant to be taking advantage of would fade before long. She pictured the roses, blowsy and dropping, almost obscene in the grey light of the summer evening.

She considered whether she could bear the indignity

of her position by bawling up the stairs for her husband, there in the front room in his chair, hearing aid turned down, asleep. She struggled to shift herself, to at least pull her skirt down from where it was bunched around her lower back. He would be useless anyway, she thought. So small, so swallowed by the world. Their flat, where she'd over the years rearranged the furniture in every possible configuration to make it more spacious, felt as vast as an airport whenever she or the carers helped him from the living room to the kitchen to the bedroom. From chair to chair to chair. The ache of seeing him so helpless she managed (too often, she knew) with a shove of revulsion as she'd done when the hospital transport didn't show last week, both on the main road waiting for a taxi. Several passed him in his wheelchair, her clutching the plastic folder with his papers, the list of medications he was on, referral letters from the GP. One of the drivers shouting apologetically from his window: *Ramp's broken, love.* She'd wanted to shake her husband then, sitting with his body curled like a cat's ear. She left him to go back indoors for the Polish cleaning woman, begging her to flag down a taxi with her uniform and her whiteness.

In the grip of this memory she struggled much more seriously, trying to stand this time, but her body could not follow the required steps, her joints had forgotten the required language. Another jolt of pain in her knee. What had she done? What if she had caused something irreparable, some damage that they could not afford? The care package from the local authority was in place, but only for him. She had no official sanction to need yet. There was a long list of things they weren't allowed to do, such as cleaning the carpet she was lying on. The carpet was "communal" and therefore *out of their remit*, she had been told, and now she tried not to think about the layers of filth being rubbed into her clothes and skin.

It had taken some getting used to, how the carers never paused for conversation, eyes on their work, strained and distracted. She urged cups of tea on them though they told her they couldn't stay, starting the kettle as soon as they came through the door to not waste their time. A quick sip if they were watched but she found the cups once they were out the door, nearly full and still warm.

When her stomach growled, she remembered the biscuit she'd put in her pocket before heading down, a snack to keep her going. At least that could come in useful, she thought. They were the young man's favourites really, not hers or her husband's. He had lived here the second longest after them, had stayed until there were greying streaks in his hair. Almost every night he'd stop upstairs after work before going into his own house, it was as if their flat was really his living room and he only went downstairs to sleep. They would watch the news together and he would be so patient and good, explaining things. There was something. If it turned out not to be love, it was respect.

After the second bite she spat the biscuit into the piece of kitchen roll. Stale. Of course it would be. The young man hadn't been back for months, despite her phoning regularly. Recently the calls consistently went to voicemail, her voice ringing out into an unknown place, shamefully loud as she reminded him how much she missed him.

They must have changed, she and her husband, into different people, people of no interest to anyone. It frightened her, how this had happened without her realising, without knowing the steps that could be taken to stop it. But she hadn't thought, when she was young, about what it would mean to marry a man fifteen years older, how cruel the change would be. Back then he smelled of coffee and cigarettes and cologne, a smell that placed him in a world of travel and opportunity, work to dress up for and long evenings talking to people who hung on his every word. She had once been a full woman to him, not just someone who wiped and assisted and arranged and resolved. His knowing, tender grin now confined to a picture frame, that shot from his mother's porch back in the mountains, propped on his table beside his chair for the carers to see. He wouldn't ask how she'd got on with the roses. Wouldn't look out the window.

It came from above her head, so loud and close, and she remembered with fresh dismay that the new neighbours were home, that only a door separated them from where she sprawled on the dirty carpet. She willed them to move away, to stay safely inside their flat, but their voices remained stubbornly close, that peal of laughter. Her fall must have been loud, her head heavy and jumbled, but their voices bubbled away cheerful and clear, the light under the door brightening suddenly as a switch snapped on somewhere, chair legs scraping across the floor.

First the voice she knew, had remembered from the day they'd moved in. It had taken all day, she thought there would be no end to the boxes. They'd looked heavy, the moving men making little *oof* noises as they heaved them up the drive. One box burst and a tower of books collapsed onto the pavement. A small dark boy darted forwards and picked them back up, reverentially, restoring them where the pages had bent and pleated. She had put on her glasses, peered closer. There was something in his fussy concern, his crouched over posture, afraid for his books in the chaos of the van and the men and their boots that made her see he was not a boy. A girl, maybe even a woman, annoyed at having her books out in the open for everyone to see. Well don't bother, she'd thought, aiming her grievance straight down at her. Nobody's interested in anything you have.

But now the voice sounded happy, and relaxed, and the replies were in the voice of another woman. There's something between them, she thought with a curiosity that surprised her, the ease with which they talked over each other in a rush to finish their sentences, punctuated by companionable silences when they chewed their food. But there was something else, a note of unmistakable tenderness that grabbed and twisted her inside.

Her legs stuck out like a doll's veins seeming to unfurl across her dark skin, blossoming into purple and deep blue. She felt something stirring inside her at the sound of these women, tentacles of a long-forgotten creature creeping from an unseen place. Her kitchen, buttery with yellow sunlight. Their first good friends in the street, the electrician and his wife, George and Carla. They'd come over the year before them, swapped place names from a lifetime ago. At church together, Carla had stood next to her and taken her arm in a sisterly way, a warm smile that nobody could question, preparing her for all that would come. The four of them walked to church on Sundays, shared dinner twice a week, lingering in each other's kitchens, went for picnics in Greenwich Park and to the seaside, with lunch pails of stew and rice. She and Carla sat at each other's tables, topping and tailing okra and green beans, sorting through grains of rice, discarding the tiny stones only they could see. What fortune to find someone to stand next to, looking out on the world, the magic of her, conjuring joy from tedium, what they had multiplied, her happiness expanding further than she could have imagined.

That happiness was behind the neighbour's door, the meal they were having together just one of the many ways in which they had chosen each other. The cooking smells, trapped above her head, were rich and garlicky. She thought of her own unprepared dinner, her husband's uninterrupted sleep. She imagined his confusion when he eventually awoke, alone in the darkened room.

Whatever had happened between her and Carla, it was never about her husband. It was never about not loving him. It was never a plan she had in her head, or a desire she'd harboured in her heart. She didn't know what was going to happen, or what she was going to do, until it happened. Until she was doing. Until that afternoon, just the two of them at her kitchen table. Instead of saying goodbye and getting up to go, Carla reached out with two fingers, and traced her brow with the same light touch you would use for a skittish, baby animal. A chick, or a rabbit.

She could have saved herself all the times they would come together in that way, of that secret-feeling, if she'd stopped there. She could have saved herself the many months of heartbreak, the dinner where George announced they were moving away, Carla serving crumble and custard, smiling brightly and not meeting her eye. She could have saved her husband trying to comfort her, thinking her distraught at losing such good neighbours. *There'll be other people.* She would finally find a way to tell him, in his often-confused state, that he was wrong. When Carla, the electrician's wife, asked: *Do you want me to take my hand away?* she could have kept her eyes open.

Closing them now, they were slippery with tears. Everything dissolved, the carpet, the stairs, the peeling wallpaper. In the blur she appeared to herself as a young woman, more clearly than she had in a long time, weary but hopeful that this flat would be the last. She wanted to reach out to herself back then, clasp her in her wrinkled hands, tell her to not want too hard, anything she had would be taken away and it was just a question of when. So absorbed in delivering this lost warning, her sobs heaving in her chest, that she did not hear the footsteps pounding towards her, so unprepared when the door opened wide and covered her in light.

Dog Days of Yoga

Bob Merckel

Barcelona

You take your mat to the park and wander around until you find a secluded spot away from the *manteros* and the kids playing football. Away from the teenagers drinking *calimocho*, a local delicacy of cheap red wine and Coca-Cola, and sway-bopping to reggaeton. Away from the yapping terriers fighting over a stick and the families with strollers.

You find a tree to crawl under, it's almost like a canopy. Someone once told you – probably Jack – that it's a Japanese spindle tree. You have no reason to doubt them, but no real reason to believe. The Borrowers would find it enormous. You feel like Gulliver in Lilliput. You're mixing your literary metaphors but that's the way your brain is working today.

So here you are, sitting under a tree. Hello, Buddha.

You arrange the mat so you'll be able to stand at the top, just outside of the canopy, but still in the shade.

You center yourself, take a deep breath in, coming into *tadasana* for a few breaths. Birds are chirping. Locals are chatting indistinctly. Children keep going where their parents tell them not to.

You raise your arms above your head and look up towards your hands, palms together in prayer position. You bend backwards ever so slightly, and you feel the tiniest of adjustments as your vertebrae click into less familiar alignment.

Swing music, the gentle jazzy kind, is playing in the distance. Barcelona is a dancing town and there's usually people in the big gazebo coming together to get their dance on. You remember that gazebo in Spanish is *glorieta*, and that this particular structure, la Glorieta de la Transexual Sonia, is in memory of a trans woman murdered here in the early 90s by a group of neo-Nazis.

"*Dios mío*," you think. "What a fucking world."

You slowly breathe out into standing forward fold and let yourself hang there for a couple of breaths, reminding yourself to drop your head and not look forward. Your hamstrings are tight. The outside of your right knee asks if you truly want to be doing this today. It's hard to straighten your legs. But everything will open up in time. Every day is different.

Breathe in, flatten your back, look forward. You step back into *chaturanga*. This is your task for today, to get to the next pose in this sequence. You're feeling sassy this morning and you had a good walk to the park so despite your complaining thighs and knee, you inhale and jump back into plank position. It is not a graceful jump. Lowering yourself down into four-limbed staff you feel your left shoulder pinch, just behind the scapula. There's a knot that you often tell massage therapists was surgically implanted to make their lives more challenging. You make a mental note to see Pedro and have him hurt you – in a good way.

You stay down here for a couple of breaths. The ground beneath the mat is softer than normal, more uneven. Despite being like literally on the ground, you feel less grounded. Or maybe you need to make a more concerted effort to ground yourself – not just because of the uneven terrain, but because of everything going on around you.

You can smell the dirt. The grass smells discernibly different than when it has been freshly cut. There's a woodsy aroma of twigs and fallen leaves coming in over the familiar rubbery scent of your mat. It smells fertile, like something you could plant yourself in and grow.

A breeze blows in from your left. Someone upwind is smoking weed.

From *chaturanga* you exhale into Upward Facing Dog. It's one of your favorite stretches. Odd how you think of this one as more of a stretch than a pose.

You push into the mat and straighten your arms to become two pillars beneath your shoulders.

Cadiz

You borrow a mat from the hotel spa and walk across the street to the park on the other side of the promenade, the one where you'll run later on today. It's full of palms and cacti. There are cypress trees and one particularly giant rubber tree (or is it a fig?). You were never good with trees, but you like doing the pose.

You unroll the mat in a corner of Parque Genovés. It's not like Park Ciutadella in Barcelona. The gazebo here looks like a spaceship, much larger than the one back home. Nobody is swing dancing, but there's a dad playing tag with his three kids and they seem to be having fun. The mat is thicker than the one you've been using, more cushion on top of the springy ground; a different give, the texture somewhat stickier than the older, more worn-down one you use at home. But the mat feels strangely familiar even though it's new to you.

It's like kissing someone new – it usually feels sort of the same, but you never know quite what to expect and it takes a while to get comfortable with the differences.

You ease yourself through the sequence of the Sun Salute.

You are a mountain surrounded by trees. The breeze is cooler than you ever thought it would be this time of year in the south of Spain. You can hear the gurgle of fountains not far away. The air smells green.

You exhale into Standing Forward Bend. It's your

first one of the day, but you realize you can go further into it than when you restarted the practice a couple of months ago. And yet here you are, restarting.

Push back into *chaturanga*, exhale back into Downward Dog. The stretch feels so good after 8 hours of train travel yesterday. It's still not a resting pose (will it ever be?), but you feel well-rested and take five breaths while pedaling one heel after the other into the mat. You think about maybe taking a bike tour and pedaling around Cadiz. Then step forward, returning into Half Standing Forward Bend. Dad is taking his kids to the fountain. You'd noticed earlier his fading commitment to the game. You are in awe of the dragon tree on the other side of the gazebo. A giant monk of a tree, its thick branches forking into smaller ones, reaching up not out, covered by a tonsure of leaves.

You breathe out and fold over into *uttanasana*. It seems easier today than yesterday, maybe because you're doing it after a lot of walking last night, first through the labyrinth of town to see the Plaza de España: is there one in every Spanish city? And why does this one feel so *tranquilo* yet monumental? Then a stroll back through the *maravilla* that is the Alomeda Apodaca with its giant fairy-tale ficuses, magnificently tiled fountains, and bougainvillea-laden trellises. Then to rest on an unexpectedly comfortable wrought-iron bench, soaking in the Atlantic breeze, trying to discern what differentiates it from the Mediterranean air you were breathing yesterday.

Your fingers splay down on the mat and you see the tiniest of beetles has joined your practice. You watch how he suddenly stops as if he's realizing "hey, this isn't grass anymore, how'd it happen?" You picture him looking around, shrugging his thorax and saying, "it is what it is" as he restarts his gentle journey to the other edge of the mat. You're so zen, you're attracting the local fauna. Next it'll be those ducks by the fountain, waddling over for a visit.

You inhale up, back into Standing Salute. It's the last inhalation of this round of Sun Salute. And you're doing it under the Andalusian sun, bright and suspended in the clearest of blue skies in a public garden you'd only heard of last week.

You cannot help but squint. Despite the chilly sea breeze, the sun warms your upstretched neck. The mat feels squishy and solid beneath your feet.

Your legs are engaged and your back arches backwards more smoothly than the first breath of today's practice.

You breathe in again, grateful for the extra breath, for the extra moment in this posture.

You exhale, lowering your arms and placing them in prayer position. One sun salutation complete. Surrounded by other yogis in a studio, you'd be doing five more of these. But here in this park amongst the trees, you lift your right foot and place it as high up as you can against the opposite inner thigh.

You engage your left thigh muscles, pushing down into the squishy solidness. You focus on something that will not move. That V where a branch of the dragon tree forks into two. Unmoved by the wind, you stand solid under his tonsure. You have your balance for now. You know it is fleeting and often takes a series of micro-adjustments to stay there. You wish you had something to hold onto as you start to lose the pose. You waver. You drop your leg. You breathe and go back into it. Your hip is still tight, but not like it was several months ago. You try to open up just a little more, to bring the knee back into a line parallel with your hipbones. Your *gluteus medias* says, "not that far." And you realize you are where you are and that's okay.

You are where you are.

You breathe.

You balance.

You are in a park surrounded by trees hundreds of years old in a city founded in 1104 BC.

You breathe into the pose. You breathe into the balance. You breathe into how short these breaths are, how old this ground is.

You slowly bring your foot down.

You place it onto this mat that isn't yours, and center yourself.

You raise your left foot up, placing your heel into the

top of your right inner thigh. There is no pain on this side, nor discomfort in your adductor as you slowly rotate it out. You are healing. You think it has taken forever, but it's just been a moment.

Your pain. Your discomfort. Your breath. Your distractions. They are just moments.

Engage the right thigh. Ground the right foot into the mat.

You breathe.

You balance.

You take in this moment of peace. You take in the fact that yesterday you were so fraught with anxiety you almost cancelled the trip.

The fountains. The traffic. The ducks. The palms. The breeze.

You hear your breath, quiet.

You breathe.

You balance.

You lower your leg. The tree becomes the mountain.

You smile and realize you are crying.

You realize you might not be that balanced.

You are where you are.

You breathe.

Tyresö, Sweden

Witham, UK

Laurenceville, NJ, USA

Madrid, Spain

Albuquerque, NM, USA

Cardiff, Wales

Toenails

Joanna Kania

I live with them. It's natural now. I couldn't imagine things like this happening when I was younger. But I needn't have worried. For every piece must fall into place before a story ends.

When John was alive, we lived in a small house in a village named Haynovka, in the north-east of Poland. We had an apple orchard on the doorstep. I have a picture of John, in black and white, on a ladder, a grey apple in his happy hand.

All my life I've loved beads. Beads and dresses. And white embroidered shirts. Skirts, too, in every colour. And scarves. I liked wearing them, enjoying people's attention. Watching out for the evil eye as well. Warding off an envious look if need be. I would savour the peace and quiet among the apple trees as John kept himself busy around the house. Our kids grew up running around with other kids from the neighbourhood.

I was the apple tree at the centre of the orchard, my

apples deepest red, turning golden if you looked long enough, irresistible. It would never occur to me to ask any mirror for reassurance. Every year, on Our Lady of Greens feast the bunch of herbs and flowers I collected was so abundant that the statue of Divine Mother's eyes gleamed as I walked down the church aisle carrying it. I prayed the rosary in gratitude. I loved beads. She knew this. And *she* loved meadows.

Nowadays, even if I stay in bed for most of the day, I urge my granddaughter May, or my daughter Mary, to dress me in nice clothes. I place my arms over the blanket from Haynovka that I insist on having on top of the sheets, whether or not my daughter approves of it. Then I smile and talk to May or to myself. It doesn't bother me at all that Mary can't make sense out of it at times. She doesn't care, anyway.

May sometimes keeps working by my side when she's had enough of her aloneness at her desk in the study that adjoins my bedroom, the way the orchard adjoined our village house. May is a story writer. Fairy tales are her thing. She says they're not only for children, if they're for them at all.

She likes to read her stories to me. Fairy tales are fine, I tell her. They remind me of my childhood. My father used to read to me at bedtime, as later my John did to Mary and Steve while I tidied up the kitchen.

I was left to do as I pleased.

There were stories around.

These days May keeps getting back to the story about the undine catching absent-minded passers-by on the edge of the forest lake. Revising it. "Whoever happens upon the waterfront at an unsuitable hour," she looks at me from over her laptop, "must pay a dire price for violating the otherworldly presence."

"She enjoys people's nails, this particular one," Mary breaks in. "They remind her of shells." She giggles after she says that. Not like someone trying to contain a mixture of fascination and fear but more like an undine would laugh. As if she had nothing to be scared of.

I've never seen Mary frightened or heard an echo of hesitation in her voice. Not when she sent May over to John and I each summer and wouldn't check up on her for the entire two months of the summer holidays. Or when we visited them in the city. Then I stayed for good when John left this realm, my soul choosing to go on for a little longer.

I've slightly gone off subject. Which feels normal now that I regularly walk to the edge of the worlds.

My impression is that May has always been happy to have me around. My own daughter doesn't care. She stays in the kitchen or retreats to her room. Or keeps watering the plants, complaining about the weather and then about the plants rotting from having been overwatered. She never finds that contradictory. I let her be this way, leaving her out to herself. Sometimes it seems to me she lives elsewhere, not under the same roof as May and I.

"I need my toenails clipped," she tells me when I come to her bedside this afternoon. "I don't want the undine to grab me by my leg and drag me under the water surface."

I tell her there's no lake near her room. We live by a canal, and that can't count as a dwelling place for undines. A family of ducks, a handful of cormorants, dogs sniffing the ground or a drunkard at some odd time is quite a different set of circumstances. Besides, we're indoors, and we can pull the blinds down at night. "We're on the safe side, granny," I assure her. My mother shrugs.

"I had a dream," grandmother says. "My toes need clipping."

"Fine," I say. "I'll clip them as soon as I finish writing. Snow White is in the middle of the forest and it's high time she started to shine with her own light. These dwarfs are too focused on mining for diamonds, you can't count on them. I need to take her out of there before the queen in disguise comes knocking on the door."

"Neither of you can do that," grandma says, giving us a looming look. "I need this special person to help me."

"Who is this special person," my mother wants to know, out of the blue. She sounds more irritated than cooperative. I sometimes wonder how come she's grandma's child. I am used to her growing impatient with grandma or me. But what I can't come to terms with is that she hardly ever wonders at things. Which makes me wonder how I could be her daughter.

"She'll let you know," grandma continues. "She'll come to our place when you call her."

And she refuses to let either of us do the job or give more hints as to the toenail clipper's whereabouts.

"Very well, mother," my mother says, rolling her eyes. "Get back to us when you can tell us more details." But granny doesn't say a word.

I search the local area over the Internet but nobody seems available. That is, a pedicurist who'd be willing to come over as it would be impossible to take grandmother anywhere.

"Leave the house and do some footwork," my mother says, looking over in my direction, and goes back to her own things.

I know it sounds crazy, this piece of advice. But I also know grandma won't give up once an idea gets stuck in her mind like that, so I put on my green coat and a scarf.

I wish I hadn't talked about the undine with her. She's getting things mixed up.

"Let me see what can be done," I say, giving her a kiss on the cheek.

As I lean over her, I catch the smell of the apple blossoms I remember from the orchard in Haynovka, back when I was a little girl.

I imagine her running down the stairs and leaving the house. No need to come over to the window to see.

As she walks down the street, I turn the city into cobblestones. The streets are narrow now, narrow and windy. Which doors lead to a pedicurist house, I hear her inquire rhetorically inside her head. What could be a clue?

There is no clue, I tell her although she can't hear me. That's the point.

She needs to get back to work as well, I catch myself thinking as she keeps getting deeper and deeper into the city maze. She's in the middle of gathering modern versions of fairytales, cutting off some elements, adding other parts that weren't there, crooking this, bending that, jumping to a new set of outcomes. Her publisher's waiting for the collection to be complete by the end of winter. This is nearly it, the onset of spring is in sight. She likes this job. She probably wants her father to be proud of her as well.

My time's shrinking.

As I think that, her mobile phone rings. I can't hear it, as she herself hardly ever does, but I feel it vibrating in her pocket.

She answers the call. I disconnect it with all the ill will I have at my disposal. Just in time. Who was that, interfering with my plan? I call her number, and she answers the call. Good.

"I can come over to do this," I say, changing my voice so that she cannot recognise me. "Clipping your grandma's nails. You just need to give me the name of the street and the house number."

Who are you would be the most obvious response.

"Who are you?" I ask.

"I can clip your grandma's nails," she laughs.

She sounds animated yet the voice does not belong to a young person, nor to someone middle-aged. Nor to anyone I know.

"Would you like me to come round to pick you up in my car?" I propose.

"No, no," she says, "I can manage. I'll take the tram."

Laughter again.

"If you wish," I say. "We live on the outskirts of the city."

I tell her the address, though I question every thing that has happened since I left the house.

"How old are you?" I ask before hanging up.

"I'm ninety-four," she says. "We need to keep that undine at bay."

"How do you," I start but she steps in between my words.

"I have to go now" is what she says. "Sleeping Beauty is bound to be waking up soon. I can see the prince climbing up the last handful of briar's cragg. Plus, the tower steps need sweeping."

Before I know it, I'm back at the doorstep to our house. Carrying a bag of apples. They don't resemble supermarket apples, nor the ones from the old greengrocer's round the corner.

May comes back with her tote bag full of apples. She puts the bag on the sheets and opens it so that I can have a look.

"I wish you could bite into one," she laughs, looking at me. "No worries, though, I'll make you an apple pie."

She's so delightful. I can see myself in her. Then I see myself as a girl, on a meadow behind the farmhouse. Then, myself in a pew, at a service for Our Lady of Greens. I look around for the statue. There she is. Her eyes gleam, and her hair smells of herbs. Before I know it, she steps off the pedestal in the side nave, walks up the main aisle and towards the church door.

She stops over the threshold.

"Follow me," she says. Her voice is irresistible. Nobody seems to have noticed a thing. As if they were all asleep.

I need to tell May, I catch myself thinking before my eyes close.

"Did you find that pedicurist?"

Mother appears at the door to grandma's bedroom. I shrug. I am caught unaware. Where have I been?

"Yes, you won't believe it," I say. "But don't ask me how. Sort of a miracle."

"Very well then," my mother says. "When is she coming?"

"In three days and three nights," I inform her. "That's what she said before disconnecting."

"That's plenty of time to sort things out," she says, more to herself than to us, and withdraws to the kitchen. I want to talk to grandma but she's fallen asleep. I tiptoe to my room.

It's getting dark.

"I need to end with the undine. The story's eating me," I say.

Mother is making breakfast.

"You said you were working on Snow White," she says. She doesn't turn as she speaks.

"The two stories sort of mixed up, fighting for my attention," I confess. I'm surprised it's my mother I'm talking to about it.

But she stays silent. I give her a look. She's still standing near the oven, making food for grandma. All I see is her back, like a forest wall, relentless, unpassable. Impossibly dark.

"Mom," I call. But I can't see her. Where she was standing there's a lake. Something moves inside its dark waters. Then grabs me by the feet. I fall.

"Granny!" I scream. Water fills my mouth and reaches further. I push, as if fighting for life. It was morning a minute ago. Now it feels like midnight. I am fighting for my life. But something stronger is fighting back.

"I couldn't come earlier," she says. I can't hear her properly because my ears are stuck with seaweed. But I recognise the voice. It's the old woman who was to come to clip grandma's toenails.

"Three days and three nights. No sooner. Someone has changed the storyline," she says.

"Who could do that?" my grandma asks.

"She did," the undine says. I can feel her moving her arm to point somewhere. But I can't open my eyes.

"Yes," I hear the other voice. "This is my story."

"How could you, Mary, daughter?" grandma wails. "How could you?"

"I cannot change this completely," the old woman says. "But I can soften it. Exchange her for someone else."

The undine's grip loosens.

"Mom!" my mother shrieks. Her voice feels as cold as ice, breaking.

Then all goes quiet.

For the first time she cries. After so many times of not crying. I hold her in my arms. She feels like a baby girl until I realise it's the other way round. I'm tiny and she's nursing me. I want to stay here until I quench this sudden hunger, this sudden thirst. I didn't realise I'd been carrying it around since I came here.

But what is *here*?

I open my eyes. We're inside a round room with a brick wall. The orange colour of the bricks feels warm. It's light as if it was summer. There's a window somewhere near as I can feel the breeze on my skin. So soft I find it almost unbearable.

"Where are we?" I hear myself asking.

"On top of the tower," the old woman says. "It's time to get back to life, Mary."

Or did she say May?

My eyes are getting heavy. I can't help it. Then I can feel her kissing my toes. Toe after toe after toe.

why? I'm not sure — perhaps because
lined with thick wool saddle pads or
quilted turnout blankets, one for each
A few from the vending machine outside
maybe a Payday bar if I had the money, a
from school as soon after the final bell
it. Western was the largest high scool in
graduating class would be, truly, the larges
le, when I finally escaped the place on Ju
never escape thing, not just the two or
rooms per week I'd tell Mom I was goin
kid's house, and instead tell them I ha
Being with the horses — especially Midge
eth's Riding Stables was just about the be
world. I'd dump my books, open the rool
-g it, then grab a curry comb and brush
idge B's stall, or into the turnout paddock
nd bring her into the central tie-up on t
g the barn. By that time, old Mr. Arnold
st about whatever I wanted. I guess he
ep and I didn't bug him. I'd muck out a st
-s of hay if there was time before I had to be
ess Mom never noticed I smelled like ho
then there was no employment law about
s it # good I never got kicked or bit there.
d decades later — when I had my own horses
rgery, watch out for bees when you're loading a
trailer, right? Right! Why am I even thinki
Arnold and Midge "B" today? I woke up an
king about Marya, I guess. She's been dead ova
ess. She was the smoker, never quit. Maybe t
day, finally, a year later! Yes, she wants T
t her grandpa I have — USMC. KIA Korea — a

A Boy with the
Same Color Hair
Valerie Fox

Mid-Life

There's Ted, he's at Al's Airport Inn. He's about forty years old in this memory. Him of the skinny black tie, drowning in the sickening sweet of a coffee martini.

"That's Ted," people sing-song. "He's a real painter." They say it without irony, it comes right out.

He stirs in people something nameless, that nevertheless adds some purpose to their days, their months, their years.

Earlier, before this particular cocktail, back in his attic studio out at the family farm, Ted had found a memento of Jason, his first love. Buried in a box of photographs, Jason's first driver's license. Age sixteen, height five foot eight, eye color brown. A slight plastic pocket contains a folded paper card. Ted can't help but touch it.

Out falls a tiny bunch of sad, brown hairs. He tosses them into a sheer green compostable trash bag, takes it out to the curb, and heads over to Al's.

That's Ted.

Happy not to have his own kids, sometimes he was available for our childcare. He might drop my sister and me off in town at the drugstore with some money for school supplies or female things, while he headed over to Iona's to catch up with his confidants. Once we went over to People's Antiques and Collectibles, where we had our own material confidants, and made up a game. These are the rules. The player who moves first is the youngest (that's me). My sister is a number of years older. Play should begin in a room full of Victoriana, ideally with *Woman in Flowered Bonnet*. Scorekeeping is Beatles-themed and seconds are tracked by a radioactive clock radio. The game is about locating and handling currency and fragile items like egos and dreams.

Over the years we may have adjusted, certainly adapted, the rules of the People's Antiques and Collectibles game. One version involves sleepy handwriting and mailing old post cards, using the addresses provided. It's a form of talking with the dead, strangers or otherwise. There's a getting-older option too, called Natural Aging in which the radio still figures prominently, laughing itself off and on and answering only to the name of our mother. Or someone called mother. This radio voice chooses the best story and the one who tells the best story gets one wish. Uncle should be here by now, but when he's not, we keep playing. If I get a wish it's to go back home. If my sister gets a wish, she asks to be taken far, far away.

An Inheritance (from Ted) Can Be More Than Just Money
1. Already at the airport, Morgana, my sister, can't find her passport, so she calls home to confirm who she is. Uncle says, "Your mother won't come to the phone." That's how our mother used to act (when someone runs away, or when they don't). Now you all know.

2. Uncle: *She has backed into her room to catch up on her ironing, napping, folding.*

3. This is just as she used to do Halloween night, especially that time when our neighborhood theme was Ancient Egypt. We had to hand out apples and bone-shaped sugar cookies since she'd been too cheap to get store-bought candy.

4. She made us write down who stopped by and what they wore and what they said.

5. Uncle: *Welcome to my underworld.*

6. We kept foot-printing King Arthur flour all over the living-room, spoiling the effect of cleanliness we hoped

to telegraph to the costumed kids who stopped by.

7. Changing the locks can only keep bad luck out for so long. Over the years, as Ted reached 50, 55, etc, he found less and less time to paint because he was caring for our mother, and also needed time to unwind at some tavern or coffeeshop.

8. Ted might get waylaid in a bookstore in the science and technology aisle, memorizing infographics and searching for Jason's name in the footnotes or the row-boat put in there for kids to play in.

9. Still, I do my part. I am always the one to do the obituaries around here when somebody dies.

10. In a Dickens book, my mother would wear an unnecessary veil and not be responsible for composing any life stories, though she was good at making brief, memorable cameos.

11. I keep Uncle in the dark though, overall. He is prone to divulge secrets.

12. His antics do appeal to both children and adults across the educational spectrum. He has riveting hand gestures.

13. Compared to Uncle Teddy I'm temperate, though we have similar tight pants.

14. Uncle: *If you concentrate real hard, you can guess where the cabinet key is hidden.*

15. He always, when he tells me about his earlier life, knows how to make the unbelievable seem natural, and the natural seem inevitable.

16. Childhood should be a natural thing, but it isn't.

17. Once there was a bright little girl with a symmetrical gaze that shone through the heavy weight of cigarette smoke and the voices chirping from her mother's soap opera soundtrack.

18. My sister and I were born in the fog of this smoke. Morgana is my sister's almost name, the name they almost gave her.

19. With us, there is always a song going on within and without, and so I listen.

20. Dear My Faraway Sister, I keep losing your copy of *Great Expectations*. Now, what will I read on the plane?

Time to Go

A painting up there in Uncle's room was called *Screech Owl* and had a scarlet line dividing left and right, inside and out. I used to climb in there with an imaginary friend, we'd find a boat to hide in and sail. We'd pretend to have a glass of wine. They had wine in there that tasted like air. I would think about that later, and think about leaving while everyone else was showing off (acting out) or watching cowboys on television. I could change my ending or the beginning but not both. When he knew it was time to go, Uncle Teddy just left, kind of dissipated, and I knew that I was the one who was supposed to be able to figure out how to operate his HAM radio, but I failed, though I kept trying.

I knew where Ted kept his important recipes and sketches, or thought I did, one can never know for sure. One drawing is called Party Favor. It's about that time Teddy rescued my sister from a party she was stranded at, it had gotten all Satanic. Envision this: she's run out of gas. It's before cell phones but somehow Morgana communicates to Uncle that she needs to be retrieved from out there. Yeah, rescued. This is deep in the woods. I'm the only one he's ever told about the origin of this sketch and why he never turned it into an epic, put it out there in the world, it being so personal. Imagine Morgana at a round table like they have at weddings and awards dinners, and coincidentally her table's theme is ESP. A man there looks like Mr. Mahoney, shifty chem teacher, except he's the opposite in every way (bleached blond hair, argyle tie, fashion boots). Or not entirely opposite, but so it seemed in the moment, at the party (to my sister). He keeps trying to hold her hand but my sister refuses to release her iron grip on her Chardonnay (bone-dry). As hinted, herein, everyone gets a newt as a gift, a party favor, like at a kids' birthday party. My sister lost hers somehow, but when I think of her (by the water, especially her California years), there is a shadowy, orange S-shape.

So there's Ted. He chose the night. It helped him remember. Before going to sleep, for hours, he'd sketch and paint some figures up in his turret, the attic room of the family farmhouse on the crap farm, hardly a castle but it held the view of his realm. He sketches and starts to remember.

When midnight comes, the world is his and ceases to mock him. He sees himself, as in a mirror, in a bar in the Village, back in his twenties. In those days he was good at disappearing and that would be the kind of place he'd run off to.

As he paints, Ted tells me things the same as he did back when I was ten. He tells me again that the story behind a name is important. In the sky there is Draco, dragon, like my mom used to be (not anymore). There is Cygnus and his companion. It means a message can take six days to go across a series of planes, or seven thousand years. There is Gemini, the boy with the same color hair, the same curve of hip. A wooden ship sailing, bound for a battle, well-equipped. Maybe it keeps you up in its vast hold, for a while.

He still names his paintings after constellations. Points arranged across the flickering, silver-gold field go a long way towards explaining so much more than a child choked in a fire, or a lost lover, or a jealous friend.

You are a constellation.

The stars up there are fixed in the sky, even though we can't always see them.

See that river. See that paw. A fish with horns. Let's go there.

Don't Hope All's Well Me

SHAUN LEVIN

He's always away: at work, with friends, out drinking, looking for sex. But I knock, I keep knocking. I know this door so well I could spot it in a crowd, approach it at a party. *Hello, Door.* Scratch marks like snail trails emerging from the key-hole (the slip of a drunken hand), sunburnt varnish peeling, a frosted glass window, thanks to which I know he's not in; I'd have spotted signs of life. I keep knocking, expecting a welcome, the slaughtering of a lamb in my honour, sizzling flesh. I have, I'll admit it, high expectations.

It's been a week. Then one day there's a postcard, as if I'd been kept in mind all along, and if only he hadn't been so busy, so very very busy, he'd be knocking at my door to be let in. Little pig, little pig. A postcard from a café in town, brought to my house, slipped through the letterbox. "Hi there, Would love to meet for coffee. Hope you're well. xxx." The café on the postcard has a yellow awning and pavement tables; it's in Camden, round the corner from his house. Once when we walked past, he'd said: Hanif Kureishi likes to sit here. I told him I had an ex who knew someone who had an affair with him, which is when he tells me that he designed Hanif Kureishi's garden. I stare at the picture hoping that when I turn the postcard over again I'll be able to read it with equanimity, especially the triple x. The xxx.

✓ = present, x = absent. Three times absent.

That sign you make when warding off the devil. X. Not kisses. X and 0 are not, as far as I'm concerned, a kiss and a hug; they're an absence and a failure. If a man wants to send kisses he must say kisses. X marks the spot where the word love used to be, and if not Love, then at least kisses.

Hi there. While he's thinking: What the fuck was his name? Or the way you do when you send a group email and say "hi there" or "hey" to express familiarity. All letters should begin: Dear so-and-so. Even the most inconsequential of notes should start with Dear ___. All you want is to hear him say your name, to know he has written your name the way as a kid you'd write your name, reaffirming your identity, your presence, or the name of someone you loved as if that name were your own. I want him to obsess but he may have forgotten my name.

A neighbour might have told him a guy with my description was knocking – day and night – which is why he figured a postcard might put an end to my knocking.

Let the poor bastard think we'll meet again. A postcard with a subtext that says: "I know you've been to my house. Now stop." At least he remembered where I live. He must have written it down the night we spoke on the phone and he came over in his car from Camden. He must have driven, chosen not to mail the postcard, because now you know he has your address and decided not to use it; he must have knocked and you weren't in, ran back to his car, jotted down a note, slipped it through the letter-box.

Would love to meet for coffee? Would love to? What happened to the I? Then the word love, lacing the statement with enthusiasm. I *love* chocolate, the little girl says. So, says the little boy, are you going to *marry* chocolate? "Would love to…" Lazy people skip pronouns. I have a friend who emails: Been thinking of you, blah blah blah, then signs off: Love you. And I think: That statement has three words to it, and anything less… it's all or fuck-all. People need to commit; there's a crisis of commitment. People need to say what they mean, not try and get away with shaved-off sentences and the illusion of intimacy; if "Love you" means "I'm not ready for any commitments but I want to pretend we're close and I'm scared of getting hurt this early on in our thing so I won't say I love you, not yet, and maybe never." Then say that. Don't hope you're well me. Show some effort, not words and phrases that hang in the air like over-ripe plums ready to splat on the ground. We are what we eat. Eat a cliché be a cliché.

A platitude, a hackneyed phrase. Don't hope you're well me. How much of a wish is there in that expression, how much genuine concern for my health and well-being?

I'm going to talk to him about this, insist on honesty and a pledge to say what we mean. If I'm insistent enough, if I knock enough, he'll eventually be there to let me in. A time will come when I knock and he'll be home and he'll open the door. He's not the type of person to hide. We have interests and pursuits in common. We even look alike. There was that moment, standing at the counter at the bar, that same night – the one and only night so far – the night we went back to my place and I looked at the two of us in the mirror and I thought: We could be related. So I leave *him* a note this time. Dear Tom. I'm well, thanks. Busy as usual. Sure, would love to meet up. Email or call when you're back and we'll arrange something. Hope you're well. Miss you. xxx

metal shelves + donated books, plant
, and but they never seemed to
the shelves of the library. There wa
many ~~books~~ anyway, not like now—
saying dusty books and obsolete kids
e-readers + laptops, but rather, this
barely valued books, was hardly a
acpe a precursor to home-schooling
pose could be good if your parents are
be Denise Levertov's. M. used to read
u or a place like that, War + Peac
wick Papers. or she'd talk with Jody
nend — still in touch? They'd talk
stairs ~~together~~ at the end of the
of bd up to the sanctuary (main one)
church. J. was beloved by all, you
her for anything. She didn't look
~~be~~ M's mother, like a throwback 7
lot of people in the town. A lot of
s, + kids, even People oy hardly had
use to be against the Vietnam
ana stole a lot of these ~~books~~. Lat
re-wrote those years. Her mother wa
of the so-called school + later
ll as more of a nurse, than a hole

s Table Mountain. Rain
ds hang heavy in the sky
her, rain clouds hang hear
where between the ground
the sky. They arrived wit
North-Wester and they're he
stay till they explode onto
homes, our washing line
pefully empty), our cars. The
d around our homes,
ady soaked from the rain
the day before and the
before and the day befor
not drink anymore.
14 and I know how to dr
convinced them to teach me
e Adults too to relieve adu
the chore of parking th
behind gates to protect
from theft or damage
e right. I parked well. Could
anyones car on our blo

The Arch

PAWEŁ LUCIAN ŁUGIEWICZ

for Charlie Dicks

Towards the end of my mother's life I began living with Charlie. At her bedside in her last weeks, my mother had said "Look after the old man, would you?" Saying yes wasn't hard, though I wondered if we'd get along and how long it would last? He'd taken me on as a child of ten, so he wasn't someone new in my life. My father had died when I was five.

At the time I said yes to my mother, it would have surprised me if Charlie had thought he'd keep going for another eight years and I certainly hadn't considered that a possibility. My mother meant everything to him, she and rugby, he did like the rugby.

This story is from the last few years of our living together in the family home. We'd had our moments of friction but we'd been in each other's lives since 1966, when they got married on my mother's birthday. We found our way, had our routines and weekly shopping trips to the supermarket or the hardware store and Ann came to clean on a Friday morning for two hours, sharing the cost. We gave each other our space. I cooked most days, and Charlie was happy to have a meal out on the other days at a favourite café Harley's where they both used to go, until it closed down, in town.

I slowly engaged more with my mother's garden and we grew together. It's the one place my head switches off completely: weeding, pruning, planting, enjoying the scents from the different shrubs and plants, evergreen jasmine, lily of the valley, phlox, summer flowering jasmine, sweet box in the dead of winter, Daphne, a bay she'd brought back from Greece, to name a few she'd gathered into her plot. Charlie was not a natural gardener, weeds or flowers were all the same to him. When he first came to live with us, under my mother's guidance, encouragement and probably some nagging, he started to work the garden, making a compost heap, growing vegetables, courgettes, spaghetti marrow, runner beans and at that time as a youngster I liked to grow broad beans, saving some for the following year's crop. Charlie took care of the tomatoes in the small lean-to greenhouse he'd put up on the back of the garage, made sure the side shoots didn't take over, so we always had robust beef tomatoes. The place was a sun trap where I'd sometimes sunbathe naked when everything was in full leaf, unseen by the neighbours.

"Greenhouse!" exclaimed my cousin Angela, who'd

lived with my parents back in the early 80s, "It's a Wendy house!"

And so it remained, a Wendy house.

"I'm very good at ignoring things," Charlie used to say, perhaps referring to some of the "things" I got up to. By which he might have been referring to my self pleasuring, given the inference in his tone. I studied to be a funeral celebrant, deciding it wasn't for me but glad I did it and I did some writing workshops at the university.

For a few years he was utterly lost and bereft without my mother, silently grieving, never letting on, but I could see how sad he was. Years back, my mother had a small arch put up over a nowhere path in the front garden and I'd started to train the evergreen jasmine over it. The arch had rusted out so I found some wooden ones online, two for the price of one, and we put one up together in the front garden. Charlie being the engineer, he didn't just stick it in the ground. We bought right angled metal spikes, non corroding ones, which he screwed into the corner of each end of the arch, then stuck them in the ground. Good and solid, stable, still there six years later when I pass the house on my way to visit old neighbours, or to town.

"Where will you put the other arch?" he asked some weeks later.

"In the back garden," I said. "Over the path."

"No!" he said, as he threw his arms up in the air. "No, no, no."

"Why not?"

"There's not enough room to get through with the garden rubbish."

It's five feet wide, plenty of room, but he wasn't having it, out came a few more reasons why not, all not really plausible. I don't think he could bring himself to tell me the real reason and I never found it out. Determined, like my mother could sometimes be with him, I dug my heals in despite the tense atmosphere, his age – 91 – and so on.

"Put it where you like!" he said vehemently, walking away from me.

I didn't think I'd win that one, but I did, unsure of what the cost was going to be.

A few weeks later, on a day he was out, I tackled the task. I got the same metal spikes and put it up exactly as we had the one in the front garden. He didn't say a thing about it. As far as I could tell he ignored it, just as he'd said he was good at doing. Weeks later, he'd gone down to the Wendy house to check on the tomatoes and feed the birds, which had been another reason why not. He wanted to be able to see the bird feeder from the kitchen window. I wanted to see them too, and said I'd make sure the arch didn't obscure the view of the feeder. Watching him from the kitchen window ambling back down the garden path, I saw him reach the arch, my arch, and stop, look down first at one corner, then the other, inspecting how I'd fixed it. I made myself scarce before he came back in, grinning to myself like a naughty but triumphant child. He never mentioned it, not once, not even in passing, nor as far as I knew to anyone else. If I'd fixed it poorly he would have said something, which is why I made sure I'd done it exactly the way he had. He was never one to praise much, if he did it came out as a back-handed compliment, or as appreciative noises, but never words.

Somewhere in the first year after he died I had the thought that the arch might have been something my mother had wanted, but he'd refused her and couldn't bring himself to say yes to me because of it.

I don't have an arch yet in my new garden, though I do have two arbors and a pergola, a raised bed for vegetables, runner beans, carrots and I've planted three apple trees, raspberry canes, blackcurrant bushes, gooseberry bushes – red and green – and a cutting from my mum's red currant bush. I've yet to get a proper Wendy house, making do with a cheap plastic one for now. I look forward to growing tomatoes, to hear him reminding me to take the side shoots out, as he used to insist I did when he could no longer do it himself.

In a psychic reading several months after he died he said he was grateful, thanked me for being there, and apologised for sometimes being too harsh. The psychic, Debs Tye-Duck online, in Wiltshire, also told me I wasn't supposed to have stayed living with him, but I had. It was gratifying to hear these messages, but I knew I'd done the right thing, holding the space for him to carry on living as long as he wanted to with the companionship and the security of that company. Which is very much how it was for me, too. I learnt to stay in one place and put down some roots, which I've always struggled to do. We had little in common and different needs from life, but we got on. If you look for it, even in relative adversity you can find good things and living with him helped me learn to differentiate myself more, to understand that he wasn't my responsibility, a little late in the day perhaps, but it comes when it comes.

And then he fell down the stairs and broke his neck in three places, damaging his spinal cord. I'd nagged him to use the stairlift, installed initially for my mother's benefit. He used to put his tool box on it to bring it down stairs.

"I want to keep my knees going for as long as I can," he'd say.

We waited two hours for an ambulance whilst blood pooled around his head. There was nothing I could do, he couldn't get up and I knew I couldn't move him. He asked for a towel under his head, which was as much as I could do to make him comfortable, sliding it gently underneath, removing his glasses. It's a horrible experience, you just wish the clock could go back and he was in the kitchen having his morning coffee, which he still hadn't had that day.

Finally the ambulance arrived, after checking him

over they told him they needed to give him an injection to stabilise the blood flow.

"Are you allergic to anything?" they asked.

"Only to falling down stairs," he said.

The hospital stitched up his forehead and pinned two of the vertebra in his neck. He was doing well for ten days, then things went awry. Towards the end of his third week in hospital – all this during the Covid lockdown in 2021 – his game was up. The hospital asked if I wanted to see him, and so my cousin Angela, she of Wendy house fame, and I went in on the Tuesday.

"Did you see what happened?" she said when we were leaving.

He'd reached for my hand first, but I hadn't noticed.

Two days later at tea time they called again. No one was around to come with me this time. I wasn't there ten minutes. I'd been up the village to the greengrocers, who all knew him and passed on their best wishes. I held his arm and his hand, and we were silent until he looked up at me.

"Go home," he said. "Go home."

I said nothing, there was nothing to say. I let go of his hand and arm, he raised it and waved goodbye, I waved back and left the room. He died the next morning. I know he'd kept going to get to the fifth of February, the day of their wedding anniversary.

We scattered his ashes last year, ten years to the day

we'd scattered my mother's ashes, in the exact same spot, under a Japanese acer in a forest she'd liked to go to, not far from where she grew up during the Second World War and where we'd had a commemorative bench installed.

Gorée Island

ZURINA SABAN

From our seats behind the captain's cabin, I see everything. The water is flat, just right for a Christ-on-the-water painting. The engine starts. The birdsong turns to whistles. Perhaps they'd been whistling all along, now increasing their pitch to compete with the engine's deep thrum. Perhaps they're telling the story of Gorée, but their language is foreign, ancient. From the boat comes a cacophony at odds with the sea's tranquillity. I sit in silence.

They are all here – people in shorts and T-shirts, ladies in elasticated pants and tank tops, rounder ladies in long-sleeved sweaters, young Chinese tourists in pale spaghetti-strapped dresses, no bras, small bags hanging from their shoulders barely reaching their elbows, local Senegalese women in multi-coloured cloth that covers everything, including their hair, a Rastafarian in tie-dyed coveralls and a woollen hat that hides his locks, another in a Nike T-shirt and shoes, hair piled in a coiled bun, and someone in a crocheted dress that reminds me of my great aunt's doilies, little islands made to protect her waxed dining table. The sun watches.

I am here without my family, sitting next to my guide, Tidiane, who is already thinking about how to make money the next day and is trying to sell me an excursion to Pink Lake. I feign distraction by looking for the birds.

Ships lie scattered on the water, some near, some merging with the horizon, suspended in a moment.

"They wait to enter the port," Tidiane says.

"So many," I say.

He explains the importance of trade from the port, of goods being unloaded and driven from Dakar to the rest of Senegal and to neighbouring countries. I wonder if they will load anything from Senegal to take to other parts of the world. I do not ask. As we glide past the ships nearest to the port, I try to see people on board, but cannot find any. The ships hover as if waiting for a painter's brush, their goods hidden deep in their steel bodies.

Gorée appears in the distance, its pastel colours seem joyful, like a resort attracting tourists for their summer vacation. The colours remind me of Bo-Kaap in Cape Town, a place where neighbours know each other and music floats through open windows into the neighbourhood. There's a vibrancy, a zest for life and laughter. I wonder if Gorée is the same.

"Only three kilometres from Dakar," Tidiane says,

"but so different," pronouncing different without the "t," resorting to his native French.

I nod and walk to the rail at the front of the ferry to watch the island draw closer, to better see the children playing on the beach by the small pier. The ferry berths. People gush from its belly, visitors in single file over a wooden plank, several locals throwing their goods over the side and onto the pier. They follow their goods in graceful jumps, their wiry legs practiced for movement. They unzip plastic or linen sacks and start the game of selling caftans, cloth bags, jewellery and *kass kass*. Tidiane finds our Gorée guide, Musa, waiting at the end of the pier with a family – grandparents, parents, two teenage girls. The older girl wears black and has a black string around her neck, the word "T-H-E-Y" spelled out on cubed white beads. The string ends just below her throat, the letters peek out above her T-shirt.

Musa speaks American, his imitation accent mixing with the accents of the Wharton students who travelled with us on the ferry and are now huddled together to take their first group selfie on the island. What stories will they tell their families about this trip? Will our stories be the same? Can they ever be?

Musa tells us that it's possible to see from one side of the island to the other.

"Just three hundred and fifty metres wide," he says.

We say nothing. I see it later, standing in the middle

of a cobbled pathway. When I look to the right, I see the ocean, to the left – the ocean.

"And nine hundred metres long."

We say nothing. Perhaps he should have told us this at the beginning, before taking us to the slave house. Perhaps then we would have had words to comment.

He speaks of forts built to protect the island from invasion. Ironic, I think, the invaders building forts to protect themselves from invasion. One of the forts is on the cliff to our right, at the edge of the island, built by the Dutch in the seventeenth century. By the 1960s it was a jail, and twenty years later – a museum. He tells us this before we visit the slave house. I understood words better then, could make sense of sentences. I look over at the Dutch fort and remember where I'm from, the Dutch had been there too, built a fort in Cape Town in the seventeenth century. One of its bastions is called Nassau. The Dutch fort here on Gorée is called Nassau. Consistency? Lack of imagination? Or perhaps the Dutch figured they didn't need to change anything since the formula for kidnapping people and trading them for profit was working. Why fix what isn't broken?

Musa points out the police station. "It used to be a chapel," he says. "The Portuguese built it in the fifteenth century."

Our group is looking at the pink police station and shaking its head in affirmation. Affirming what? That the missionaries built churches? That is not what I am thinking. I'm thinking that not enough people prayed, but many committed crimes so the State expropriated the church. I'm thinking about the irony of using it as a police station today and not a restaurant or a shop, or to state the obvious, a church. I'm thinking about the interchangeability of houses of incarceration and prayer, and whether churches are prisons. I'm thinking about how religion is sometimes used to oppress, that men get carried away speaking for God, opining on what He wants and does not want so that they soon forget they are men and think they are God and have the right to inflict harm on others and blame those acts on God. I'm thinking that it's dangerous to think for God.

"Gorée has around twenty-eight slave houses," Musa says. "Some are now homes."

As we walk down narrow roads to the slave house, the absence of cars gives Gorée an air of being forgotten. It does not have an air of being undiscovered, because it was discovered and used for a specific purpose for centuries. As a UNESCO heritage site, the buildings are preserved aesthetically, frozen in time. The right to renovate or paint is regulated, the colour palette stuck in the shameful past of slave traders. White, pink and yellow. Flowering bougainvillea spill over colour-compliant walls, eager to watch visitors ambling down the pathways.

Even though a ferry load of people disembarked and

will continue to disembark every hour, the island feels quiet. Are we talking in hushed tones?

We enter the wooden gates to the slave house. The walls are pink, Portuguese Pink, like the police station. White is for the Dutch. I wonder why the slave house is not white since I'm told the Dutch built it in 1776. The family touring with us is English. They have history on this island. The British owned the island from 1758 to 1763 and again from 1779 to 1783. They do not have their own colour. I wonder if it mattered to the slaves which country controlled the island. British, Dutch, French, Portuguese – is it not all the same if they did the same?

On either side of the entrance, curved concrete steps go up to a balcony.

"That's where they stood," Musa says. "And where we're standing is where the slaves would be standing, naked except for a loin cloth, waiting to be examined like animals." I look at our little group. All of us are clothed. I wonder what the almost naked ladies will feel when they stand here. Perhaps their "almost naked" represents their freedom. And the Senegalese, how do they symbolize their freedom? Is this why the Senegalese ladies are covered? Is "almost naked" too close to their slave past?

We stand at the entrance, internalizing the dusty courtyard, the curved concrete steps, the entrance under the balcony that leads into the dark interior, the exit at the other end of the darkness. Musa points to that exit, "that doorway in front of you is the door of no return," he says.

It has a green door. Who owned green? Through the door and beyond the house's darkness I see the sun's light glistening on the calm sea.

"Let's have a look at the rooms first," he says, "we'll have a closer look at the door after."

Only later will I appreciate the sequencing.

Musa leads us from room to room, all five of them basic: thick, aged, stone walls, uneven sandy floors, one ceiling too low to stand up. I do not go in there. Here a room for the women. There a room for the men. Another for children under the age of twelve.

"They were kept here for up to three months," Musa says.

He shows us a room called a feedlot, where men were fattened with black-eyed beans ground into a paste. Before I can ask, Musa tells us the men were taken to the toilet once a day. My stomach knots and I am suddenly aware of my breathing – hasty exhales as if my nose does not want the air from this room. I know once a day is not enough. The room now feels smaller, darker, more disgusting. Did I really need to consider the toilet to grasp the depth of the cruelty, how people were fed legumes to draw them closer to the end of their lives?

Musa tells us that virgins could fetch a price four times higher than other women, and were separated from them. Strangely, that makes sense. Perhaps I'd heard it before.

Ripening breasts are a strong aphrodisiac. A pregnant girl could remain on the island until she gave birth and enjoyed other freedoms during this period.

"Mulatto children got additional rights," he says. "At the end of slavery, they had the right to return to France."

I wonder how the French welcomed their African offspring, whether they gave them equal rights, bread, how they treat them today. I know the answers. Still, in the belly of the slave house, I hope for different ones, the way a child longs for soothing words. I know that slavery was abolished twice in France. First in 1794, then brought back on the insistence of Napoleon's Josephine, who owned plantations. It was abolished a second time in 1848. I wish I did not know this. Being labelled "free," only to be relabelled "slave." Can you unsee freedom, unfeel it? Should I be ashamed to know the name of Napoleon's wife and not those of the people sold on this island?

"These rooms seem dark now," says Musa, "but let me remind you that the windows you see were made when the house became a museum. It had no windows when the slaves were here. The only air came from that door, which was barred with an iron grille."

Millions of people were sorted in Gorée. Sorted to determine their price and destination. Musa says up to two hundred people were held at this slave house at one time. The largest room is less than three square metres. I can see they must have lived in their own urine and faeces, their bodies in agony, their minds tormented. Children crying, women crying, virgins crying. And the men?

Musa shows us the cell for the "recalcitrant," less than a metre wide and a few metres long, too low for standing, intended for one prisoner but often used to hold a dozen. A prison within a prison, men lying on top of each other, cramped into this cave-like space. "Stacked like sardines," he says, repeating the phrase as if we did not hear him the first time or perhaps he thinks we did not understand. I know these men did not cry. A "recalcitrant" man seeks dignity and fights for his family, his right to life. A "recalcitrant" man tries, even when he knows he cannot win. This man dreams of the remembered pleasure of freedom, of his home where he lived with others, understood the take and give of honouring the land, of his family who escaped capture and are still free. He prays that it remains that way. He hears the birdsong over the children crying, the women crying, the virgins crying, hears the sea's hush, the worry of the men lying in front of him, behind him, on top of him. Like sardines. Feels their worry permeate his skin, smells it on the stale breath hovering in the darkness. In this room where he saw life most clearly, where there is no subtext or nuance, where grown men die and undie moment by moment, I know he imagines returning and living in the world again. This is what makes him "recalcitrant." In him, fear and hope are alive together and do not give birth to despair.

We are finally at "the door of no return," the doorway in the slave house from which a gangway would be placed so men and women could walk directly onto the boats that would row them to the bigger ships waiting in deeper water. Musa gives each of us a chance to experience the doorway. I stand in it, the sea stretched before me, its beauty magnificent, its power palpable. It feels expectant and looks like a glassy blue iris. I cannot see its pupil lurking in the depths, watching. But I feel it sees me, standing alone, on the last footstep of African earth. One giant swell and it could eat me. In the face of this confrontation, there is no sound. I hear nothing. No waves splashing, no people talking, no chatter, no laughter. No birds whistling. I stand here alone in this doorway, the gangway before me. Should I board the boat or should I dive into the sea and hope to drown myself with the weighted five-kilogram ball chained to my ankles. Or should I pray for the bullets from the soldiers' musket to strike my head? For a shark to swallow me whole?

Is that really the moment of death, the drowning, the musket round, the shark? Or did they die, truly die, before, sitting in faeces, waiting for that telling moment when they realised they would never return to their homes, their families, their tribe? When they walked into the slave house? When families were separated and sent to different parts of the Americas, never to see each other again? When they lost their names? Should we be grateful for being born in this time? Do the answers depend on the colour of your skin?

I am not white. My answers are clear. The damp rises stronger in my nose, the dark seems darker. When they learned about the church and the European god, did they think this place was hell, that it was the doorway to hell and that hell was made of water? I wonder if we have evolved as humans, if we are doing better now. Millions went through this island, the sorting centre. Millions suffer today, drowning in the Mediterranean, drowning in the Gulf of Mexico, starving on coastlines, waiting to be seen, possibly saved. I know there are still holding pens, sorting centres. We all know this.

"Where is the mosque?" I ask Tidiane.

He takes me three hundred metres to the other side of the island. The mosque is on a cliff, facing the sea. It is small. It is alone. A goat scampers out of its courtyard. I wash my hands, face, arms, ears, feet at the tap outside, with the goat, the sea, the sky and the birds as witnesses. To the sound of water lapping, soothing, behind my back, I pray. I say a prayer for everything. I say a prayer of thanks that I am free. I say a prayer for people who are not free. I say a prayer for the oppressors, pleading that they will discover their humanity.

We walk back to the pier. I order fish, Dorado, at the restaurant closest to the water. A Senegalese woman grills it on an open fire, presents it whole with French fries on the side. It looks appetizing. I like Dorado, take a bite, but my throat is closed, still choking on questions. I cannot eat. I sit at the square wooden table, look out to the sea. The European family is at the table in front of me, the T-H-E-Y girl faces me. I take out my notebook but only one word flows from my pen: they, they, they, they.

Tidiane and I board the next ferry back to Dakar. It is full, though less busy than the original journey. Some of the local vendors are returning too. Many passengers sit silent, exhausted by knowledge, by the meal, by the walk around the island. One local has several pairs of *kass kass*. The percussion shakers are made from large, dried seed pods filled with rice. Two pods joined by a short string makes one instrument. Several pairs of *kass kass* hang from his belt. He sees me looking and comes over, offers me a pair, which I take, aware that I will have to buy them once they are in my hand. He shows me how to drape the string through my fingers, cup a pod in the palm of each hand, leaving the attached second pod hanging down toward my feet. He shows me how to produce a sound. I try and fail. He smiles and tells me to try again. I try again and fail.

"Like this," he says and shows me slowly how to twist my wrist.

I imitate the movement, twist my wrist, the *kass kass* hanging toward my feet flies up to meet its partner in my palm. We hear the clack as they bounce against each other. He laughs and nods, "There," he says. "You've got it." I try again until I produce a clack, clack, accompanied with the sh, sh of the rice trapped in the pod's belly. He tells me the price. I know it's high, but pay without bargaining. I put them in the dark bowels of a Senegalese cloth bag I'd bought the day before. As we leave the port, he takes two, one in each hand, and starts to play. We all turn to the sh, sh, the clack clack, when he starts to sing Shakira's "Waka Waka." The song reminds me of being home in Cape Town. It reminds me of South Africa hosting the soccer World Cup. It reminds me of the thousands who visited and then went home. His voice is soft, raspy, a laboured sound pulled from his lungs into the light. The people on the ferry grow quiet. The birds are quiet. His voice grows bolder, flowers into something tactile. It rubs against my hands resting on my lap. It strokes my head now warmed by the sun. The engine's thrum is deep, almost a groan. The ferry's nose points to Dakar, toward the port, where I know my family is waiting. A gentle breeze plays with my hair. I close my eyes, tilt my face up to meet the sun.

e roamed as far as we could in the
an hour. But the hey was always
end too much time, to not return to t
ce too often / like cats. Somebody's parent might be
d if that was the case we would.
say as little as possible, be guided b
iend in how much should or should
vealed. In the bedroom, or the living roor
ody was home, lumpy spliffs were rolle
ingly polished coffee tables, as one frie
d their siblings smiled from their child
tographs. Somebody was driving the short jor
the slightly bigger shop, returning with
za slices or sausage rolls. It was summer
y going and going fish + chips for hours, always spo
ther chapter when it was time to move on
the weeks passed, it was more likely tha
ent would be home, discouraging illicit
tivity up to a point, ordering us back to
roof. Not all of us made it.
t of their l

About the Writers

Valerie Fox is a poet and fiction writer. Her poetry books include *The Rorschach Factory*, *The Glass Book*, and *Insomniatic*. Her work has appeared in the *Best Small Fictions* and *Best Microfiction* series, as well as *The Group of Seven Reimagined: Contemporary Stories Inspired by Historic Canadian Paintings*. With visual artist Jacklynn Niemiec, Valerie created *The Real Sky*, a collaborative artists book in an edition of 26 handmade copies. She co-authored, with Lynn Levin, *Poems for the Writing: Prompts for Poets*. She's taught writing at Drexel University (in Philadelphia), including with Writers Room, and at Sophia University (in Tokyo). @valeriefoxpftw

Pia Goddard is a London-based writer, photographer and multidisciplinary artist. She performs with the Rye Poets and Southwark Stanza, and has exhibited with South London Women Artists. Her writing has appeared in *Magma*, *Not Very Quiet*, *Spelt*, *ArtVerve* and *Positive Nation* magazine.

She has worked in bookshops, education, journalism, as a translator, a curator, and has run her own gallery. Her first job was for the Magic Bus Travel Company in the 1980s and she currently works part-time in a local haberdashery shop. @agulpofmagpies @ryepoets

Joyce Hertzoff has published eight books including her novella *A Bite of the Apple*, which won the New Mexico Presswomen's prize in 2016 in the young adult category and was second in the national contest. Her stories have been included in anthologies. Fiction is her reaction to forty-five years in the scientific publishing field as a translator from French, German, and Russian, and to managing large groups of scientists. She facilitates classes and mentors new students for the Writers Village University MFA program, and serves as Managing Editor for Fiction for WVU's ezine *The Village Square*. joycehertzoffauthor.com

Joanna Kania is a Poland-based niche writer delighting in poetry, fairy tale and short short fiction. Her poem appeared in *Singing in the Dark, A Global Anthology of Poetry under Lockdown*, and her essay was published at pendemic.ie. In 2023 she undertook a year-long project to write a poem a day, switching to microstories in 2024. She teaches English at OLPI/LSP in Gdansk, weaving poetry and creative writing into the curriculum, and cooperates with CSN Calma, a teachers' training centre.

She once worked in a small eccentric clothes shop in the Lake District, UK and travelled solo across the USA by train and Greyhound buses in 2000.

Shaun Levin is a writer and artist based in Madrid. His books include *Seven Sweet Things*, *Alone with a Man in a Room*, and *Snapshots of The Boy*. His creative writing courses are available on Domestika. @shaunlevin shaunlevin.com

Paweł Lucian Ługiewicz has worked mostly in hospitality of one kind or another, largely in London for thirty years. Catering jobs to office management, via working as a bus conductor and in a bookshop. He learnt his trade with Whitbread Trophy Taverns in Cardiff, where he was born and now lives. He has traveled and lived in the USA and Australia. Creatively writing for 26 years he writes memoir and fiction. Published in 2003 in the anthology *Four Seasons In A Day*, he finds respite in gardens, gardening and nature. @pav.diff

SJ Lyon is a London-based queer writer of memoir, narrative non-fiction and fiction. They were shortlisted for Spread the Word's Life Writing Prize in 2021 for "People that Might Be Us," a personal essay about queer birthdays They were selected for the London Writers Awards in 2022 to develop their first book *My Ex-Dad* about family estrangement. SJ's "Did You Know You

Can Swim in the Morning," a piece about returning to Beirut with their mother, was recently published in the creative non-fiction journal *Hinterland*. They are also a charity worker, visual artist and gardener.

Bob Merckel is a writer, editor, and language teacher who spends his time between Barcelona and Provincetown. He holds an MA in Creative Writing (Novels) from City University London. His work appears in the anthologies *Tales of the DeConstructed*, *Shaggy Blog Stories*, and *Your Messages*, amongst others. He writes and edits fiction and CNF as @bob-merckel at Medium. After leaving Ohio to tend bar in New Orleans, guard geysers in Yellowstone National Park, act off-off Broadway, and manage an international asset management firm's marketing communications, he now happily teaches English at a Catalan university. @bobzyeruncle

Cynthia Saunders Reed is an American author/editor currently living in Sweden. Previously, she's lived/worked in Thailand, the United Kingdom, France and Malaysia. A former technical and marketing author, current projects include a collection of linked historical short stories and a novel about the Crimean War. She's also editing a Young Adult novel for an autism awareness project. Her writing has appeared in *Sobotka Literary Magazine* (US), as well as in online publications, anthologies and magazines in

Europe and Asia. Now finalising an MFA Certificate in Fiction through Writer's Village University (online) she mentors international students and facilitates classes there. @UKCynthiaR, cynthiareed.substack.com

Zurina Saban writes fiction, non-fiction and poetry. Her writing has appeared in several publications, including Alice LaPlante's *Write Yourself out of a Corner*. Her work is inspired by her experiences growing up on the Cape Flats in South Africa. She lives in Morocco and has also lived in Egypt, England, Turkey and the USA. Living abroad, she initially wrote books for her children to deepen a connection between them and Africa, introducing them to local cultures, languages and faces. *Baby Thabo*, a story she wrote when they were babies, is still their most treasured book.

Ann Tudor shares her time between Shrewsbury and the Isles of Scilly. She was shortlisted for the Retreat West Micro Fiction Contest and has a diploma from Oxford University in Creative Writing. She enjoys writing the shortest of short stories, and has also drafted two novels. Her work explores everyday family relationships. As an accountant, Ann works primarily with healthcare professionals, and has written two manuals on the subject, one of which won a British Medical Association award. She is currently involved in an £18m project to establish a new museum and cultural centre on the Isles of Scilly. anntudor.co.uk

Rachel Wolcott is a financial journalist and podcaster for Thomson Reuters in London. In 2023 she exposed how Colombian drug cartels laundered money through the UK Post Office and retail banks. She has written for Euromoney magazine and other financial titles. She started her career in high school as a sports writer for the Wilton Bulletin, which paid her by the column inch. After twenty some years she is still figuring out how to live in the UK with an American accent. Rachel's fiction is about identity, memory and loss.

Holly Woodward is a writer and artist in Costa Rica. She served as writer in residence at St. Albans, Washington National Cathedral, and won the Rachel Wetzsteon Prize from the 92nd Street Y in New York. Her poems and stories appear in literary magazines on and off the web. Holly is grateful to Richard Price, Russell Banks, and Edmund White at Columbia, F. D. Reeve at Wesleyan's College of Letters, and her Ph.D. director, Larry Woiwode. Her book, *Sin for Beginners*, was finalist for the National Poetry Series. A chapbook, *Read Whatever You Want into This* is forthcoming. X: @HollyWoodward, IG: @Woodward.Holly

either Ashes or Lupo's. At Ashes [...]
[...]ce to sit. He was more handsome, I can[...]
[...]ber if he or his wife, maybe a cook he [...]
[...] the omelettes, but it was Ashe's — his [...]
[...]t the entrance to the art school, the s[...]
[...] ours. I went there mainly with [...]
[...]e I always went with her, maybe she [...]
[...]ffair with him, she had sex with a lot [...]
[...](maybe from her I learnt the joy of pro[...]
[...]. The other place was Lupo's. It was sm[...]
[...]ore than a kitchen in a kind of box, [...]
[...]today when I make an omelette fried i[...]
[...]flower oil, the smell of it — it's to Lupo[...]
[...]m that the smell takes me back to.
[...]ith or without hair?" "he or his wife [...]
Lupo →

[...]'t remember if I had hot sauce on [...]
[...]tte, fried, crispy, hugged by a while
[...]ft white bread soaking up the oil 4 [...]
[...]tte. That was lunch. We'd queue up. [...]
[...] café, watch him and his wife frying
[...]ettes and small ~~electr~~ gas cooker. The[...]
[...] brusk, miserable people, Romanians. As
[...] friendly, handsome, muscled, [...]

The story of ~~John~~ John's ice cream parlor — As a junior and senior in high school, I attended most of my classes in the morning and ju[st] a couple after lunch. Afterwards, [a] few friends and I would walk [a] mile to John's, an old fashioned ice cream parlor. winter & summer. Usually, they [had] at least eight flavors each day [li]ke twenty- ~~something~~ nine a few more [m]odern places have. ~~th~~ My favor[ite] was raspberry chocolate chip — huge da[rk] chocolate chips in raspberry-inf[used] ice cream. The cold treat wasn['t] sweet like their ~~strawberry~~ ice c[ream]. [O]r I'd have a black-and-wh[ite] chocolate soda with vanilla ice cream floating in it. We'd